Murder in the Fairy Ring

BOOK TWO IN THE ERIN'S GLEN MYSTERY SERIES

A.P. RYAN

GLENSIDE BOOKS

Copyright © 2024 by A.P. Ryan

All rights reserved. This publication, in its entirety, is protected by copyright law. It is strictly prohibited to reproduce, distribute, or transmit any part of this work in any form or by any means, including photocopying, recording, or other electronic or mechanical methods, without the prior written permission of the publisher. The only exceptions are brief quotations for critical reviews and specific noncommercial uses permitted by copyright law. For permission requests, kindly direct your inquiries to Glenside Books, Devon, UK publisher.

This is a work of fiction. Any similarities between characters and persons, living or dead, are unintentional and coincidental. Erin's Glen and many locations referred to in the book are fictitious. Some other places will be familiar, but time and imagination will have altered them.

Please note that the plant Banshees' Bloom and the band The Puffins and their song Earth Fairy are fictitious.

Contents

1. Astray — 1
2. Change in the Air — 6
3. Rosie's Rant — 10
4. Time for Tea — 15
5. Hot News — 20
6. Quinn's Curiosities — 27
7. Newsround — 32
8. An Elemental Discovery — 38
9. A Dark Morning — 43
10. Shocking News — 47
11. Craft, Cake and Conversation — 52
12. Nightmares in the Woods — 59
13. Stirring Memories — 63
14. Protests — 69

15.	Sharing Knowledge	74
16.	More Questions than Answers	78
17.	Voices from the Past	83
18.	Invasion of Privacy	88
19.	School Days	93
20.	Mysterious Disappearances	99
21.	Haunted	103
22.	Father's Confessions	108
23.	Paper Trails	113
24.	Technology Old and New	119
25.	Blaney's Blarney	125
26.	Cause of Death	130
27.	Covert Surveillance	135
28.	Information, Communication and Technology	140
29.	No Kidding	143
30.	Echoes from the Past	147
31.	In the Clear	152
32.	That Monday Morning Feeling	156
33.	Blues and Twos	163
34.	Stitch Up	167
35.	Good News	174
36.	Making connections	178
37.	Home	181
38.	Midnight Meditations	184

| 39. | One Year Later | 197 |
| 40. | Revelations, Reunions and Retreats | 207 |

Chapter One

Astray

The night was inky black. A thick layer of cloud obscured the stars that usually twinkled over Erin's Glen. A wispy veil of mist hovered close to the ground and seemed to be rising as the darkness closed in. Toddy lived a way out of the town and had a long walk back home to his dilapidated cottage in the woods. Half an hour earlier, he had left the Shenanigans Pub in town with a gaggle of other locals. The guards were about, and the proprietor of this drinking establishment wanted to hold onto his license, so he called last orders and moved the crowd out onto the street just before 11 pm.

Toddy had begun his journey shiny-faced and bleary-eyed, still giggling and hiccupping. He had been slightly unsteady on his feet but stable enough to walk the few miles home. A few of his drinking pals called out cheery goodbyes and mild jocular insults as they went their separate ways on the road out of town. It was mid-week, and after the struggle of drinkers had dispersed, a silence had crept over the street. The shop sign for Quinn's Curiosities, the antique store on the high street, creaked in the wind that now whistled along the street. A few streetlights blinked. Toddy turned up his collar and shook his cap out of his pocket. He pulled it over his unruly black curly hair and grimaced as the breeze picked up with a damp, chill edge.

'Onwards and upwards,' he murmured as he plodded up the street towards the fairy ring and home.

Toddy didn't relish his return to his squalid home. He had lived in the cottage all his life, and now that his parents had passed on, he was there alone. He had taken it upon himself to be an unofficial custodian of the fairy ring and felt that his presence was needed to protect the ancient site. His father had told him how this duty was in the family, passed on from father to son down the generations. However, the pay for this self-appointed role was non-existent, and Toddy had to make do with state handouts based on his claims of poor health, supplemented by a poached rabbit and homegrown vegetables for many of his meals. Despite his material poverty, he had a sense of purpose and an iron-clad belief in the *Shee* or little people that inhabited the sacred mound he protected.

As Toddy left the environs of the town tonight, the darkness intensified. He passed the old stone that marked the entry into the town of Erin's Glen and glanced down at it. He could barely make it out. The mist started to swirl about his legs and seemed to be creeping up his body as he walked briskly along. His pace had quickened, and his gait had levelled out now that he had sobered up in the frigid night air. He looked up, expecting to see some stars as he left behind the lights of the town, but the sky was a heavy, cloudy-black dome above his head, moonless and starless. Toddy had no torch but wasn't too concerned; he knew the route home well. He had walked it thousands of times, first with his parents and school pals and now, as an adult, increasingly solitary. He knew he was considered an oddity in the town but accepted it as part of his role.

His life now had few immediate ties with the local community. The bonds that brought people together in the town, such as church, school, sports and shopping, were not a regular part of his existence. He wasn't one for 'kissing the altar gates' as his mother used to put it; he didn't go near the church. He had no family now, and due to his bad health as a child and adolescent, he played no sports. Most weeks, his only trip into town was to venture down to Shenanigans mid-week to take advantage of the cheap drinks. Fortified by a few Guinness, he would latch on to a crowd there, usually hovering on the edge. He had learned the script of what to say – the usual jokes, jibes and nicknames that he and the others used every time they saw each other. It was a jovial social shorthand that obliterated the need for any proper conversation. That suited him. He didn't want any intrusive questions. But the men he exchanged banter with, the grown boys he went to school with, now had families of their own and jobs to go to. All Toddy had was his cottage and his position of watcher and keeper of the fairy ring.

As he rolled these thoughts around in his mind, familiar musings, he became conscious of the mist getting denser as he left the town, now a long way behind him. He put his hand out in front of him and couldn't see it. He felt his levels of anxiety rise due to the dark closing in around him, rendering him blind as he walked home on his own. He could hear the river gushing along in the darkness and was gripped by an almost primal phobia of falling into the depths of the sub-zero water. Toddy couldn't swim, and nightmares of drowning haunted him. Bad dreams troubled him more recently, isolated as he was in his cottage at night.

Toddy lifted his feet with increased awareness as he walked on. He stamped each foot down with a sense of purpose. He could feel the road beneath his feet and hear the thud of his boots on the tarmac. The land was his home, and his intuitive closeness to the earth soothed him. With a countryman's sense of direction and knowledge of the landscape, he knew where the river was in relation to the road. 'No chance of me falling in like some townie eegit.' He comforted himself with these thoughts and concentrated on the rhythmic sound of his steps along the road.

After a few paces, he stopped.

The usual landmarks, the trees, hedges, walls, mounds of earth, and the well he looked for as his two-mile marker out of town had all disappeared. Toddy felt a vertigo-like sensation sweep over him and thought he might fall to the road. His innate sense of direction was gone. He turned around, then around again. A sick, icy panic knotted in his stomach and seeped up through his intestines into his chest and spread out into his limbs. He felt jittery and disorientated by the lack of his inner compass, which usually functioned so well. He stood in the murky, misty darkness, frozen to the spot. He was confused by the sudden disappearance of the external landmarks that he usually used as his guide.

Toddy took a breath and shook himself. He strode forward in a futile attempt to regain his confidence and sense of direction. He stopped again and listened. Yes, he was sure of it now. He could hear a clip-clop behind him.

He stopped, and it stopped.

He walked on a few paces; there it was again.

Clip clop, clip clop.

He stopped abruptly, his body tense with fear and cold.

Silence.

He stood stationary, frozen by a sudden terror in the claustrophobic darkness. He could feel the tendrils of mist creep along his cheek like fingers. The fog surrounded him and hovered, silent and brooding as he waited. Toddy could hear his raspy breathing. In the distance, an owl hooted.

He gritted his teeth and strode on resolutely.

The clip-clop started again. It seemed to be following him; he quickened his pace, and it got quicker. Toddy ran and stumbled into the grass verge at the side of the road, unable to make out where the road ended and the fields began. He tripped up in the thick, long grass and fell heavily into the wet foliage. His old, broken boots had let in the wet from the grass, and he swore as his feet became soggy. As he lay shivering in the grass, he could hear the hungry gushing of the river closer now. He swallowed hard. The knot of panic now wedged in his throat, he called out hoarsely, 'Who is it?'

No answer.

Chapter Two

Change in the Air

The spring sunshine splintered the bare trees. The wooded area, sheltered by a circle of green hills and the mountain in the distance, was quiet and still. A few songbirds, returned from their winter sojourn, made a distinctive chiff-chaff sound in the distance. Ziggy, a curly-haired chocolate-coloured spaniel, scampered ahead of Rosie, a neat grey-haired lady dressed in Wellington boots and a heavy tweed coat. Rosie loved mornings like this. She smiled as she tilted her head to feel the warmth of the gentle sunshine on her face.

Over the winter, these woods had often been under a blanket of snow, but now enticed by the warmth of spring, tiny emerald shoots appeared. The daffodils provided splashes of golden colour, and Rosie spotted some early bluebells. The trees, so recently bare and stark, were now adorned with unfurling green buds. A sense of awakening and renewal was in the air. After a difficult few months over the winter, Rosie's heart began to warm with a sense of hope.

A few puffy white clouds drifted across the pure blue sky. The air sparkled with a crystal-clear freshness unique to Erin's Glen. Everything felt alive, and the sunshine sparkled off the young green leaves. Rosie paused and breathed in the sharp pine scent of the wood, her fingers brushing the rough textured bark of an oak tree she was standing by.

Suddenly, her attention was drawn to the spot where Ziggy had decided to stop abruptly. A poster was pinned to a tree. At first, Rosie was almost pained to see the trunk punctured in this way, but as she drew nearer, her attention was drawn to the content of the notice:

Please be advised that planning permission is being sought to build in this area. This site has been identified as a prime spot for an international tourist interpretation centre. The proposed centre will attract millions of visitors each year and help them understand and enjoy this area's folklore, history, and culture.

If you have any comments on this proposed development, please contact Erin's Glen Planning Permission Office.

Rosie stood stunned. She was horrified that this sacred spot would be disturbed in such a rapacious way.

Ziggy was looking intently at his mistress. His head cocked to one side with a quizzical expression on his fuzzy face. Rosie caught his eye and tutted, 'Just you wait and see; no good will come of this.'

With a deep sigh, she walked through the woods, Ziggy now scampering ahead. As she walked along thoughtfully, she caught a glimpse of something white just on the edge of her vision. She stopped to look more carefully. Rosie was able to make out a figure in the woods in the distance. It was just fleeting.

Ziggy ran off to greet the person draped in white and carrying a basket. Rosie hurried after her nosey dog, curious to catch up with the enigmatic figure. She could hear a female voice, light and tinkly, greet her canine companion. The new spring growth in the woods obscured her view, and Rosie had to rely on her sense of hearing to locate the mysterious voice. Then Rosie heard Ziggy make a noise that was halfway between a yelp of pain and a bark. A sudden panic gripped Rosie. She moved as quickly as she could through the wooded area but had to tread carefully to avoid tripping over tree roots and branches that had come down in the recent late winter storms. A low-hanging cobweb caught Rosie in the face. With frustration, she had to stop to clear off the sticky threads that clung to her features and obscured her glasses. The tinkly voice stopped, and Rosie looked this way and that, trying to decide on her route.

Ziggy came scampering back, barking at her as if to say, 'Where have you been?' He stood close to her, shivering. Rosie could feel him trembling as he leaned in against her leg. She bent over and smoothed her hand over his back, partly to reassure herself he was unharmed and partly to calm him down.

'Mmph, where have you been, young man?' Rosie replied. 'And who have you been talking to?'

Ziggy sat down and blinked at her, his amber eyes glowing in the low sunshine of the early spring morning. Rosie was unsettled by his behaviour but tried to shake off her discomfort. The little dog's shallow breath slowed, and Rosie and Ziggy continued their walk through the fairy ring wood, but this time in the direction of home. The wood was on the edge of the small town of Erin's Glen, where Rosie had lived all her life. Today, Saturday, was a day off from her job as Parish Secretary at St Brigid's church in the town, and she savoured every moment of her walk through the picturesque woods.

The sun created dappled patterns on the forest floor, and the crunch of her feet through the leaves provided a background sound to the mental chatter in Rosie's head that morning. A lot had been going on in Erin's Glen, and there had been dramatic changes over the past couple of months. Not least, a change of boss. Father Gerard, the priest she had worked with for decades, was now gone, replaced by a younger man with some strange ideas. At least as far as Rosie was concerned. The many changes in Erin's Glen unsettled her, and she had much to think about on these walks. She had taken to coming through the woods now that the weather had improved and the days were longer. It was deeply unsettling to see news that even the fort itself, an ancient monument that had been in existence for millennia, was not immune to the effects of change and so-called progress. Before leaving the woods, she turned around and looked at the hill fort. The mound dominated the woods. The grassy banks were ringed by terraced walls and ramparts. The steep curve of the convex hill rose to a flat surface on which a majestic oak tree flourished. The locals called it 'The fairy ring,' and many believed that the little folk inhabited the mound's interior. Rosie pursed her lips and sighed. She intuitively sensed it would cause trouble.

Rosie returned from the woods along a country path that opened into a sparsely housed residential area. Her small, neat bungalow was at the end of the road on the way back towards town. Its tidy garden, floral curtains and freshly painted door welcomed her home.

As she put the key in the door and stepped inside, a tall figure loomed behind her, creating a shadow in the early morning sunlight. She felt a hand on her shoulder before she turned around.

'Good morning, Rosie.'

Chapter Three

Rosie's Rant

'Oh, dear God, don't creep up on me like that!' Rosie chided her longtime friend Mary Jo.

Mary Jo – or Sister Mary Joseph – was setting off for an early morning run. A Carmelite nun living locally, she worked as a Physical Education teacher at the local school. She was often out and about walking briskly, jogging or even swimming in the river that ran through Erin's Glen.

'Ah, Rosie, I'm sorry; I just wanted to catch you quickly to ask if you heard the news.'

Both women entered the hall of Rosie's bungalow; Rosie deftly got out of her coat and boots and undid Ziggy's collar as she answered. 'I saw a notice up in the forest about planning permission for an interpretation centre. What do you make of it?'

As usual, Rosie put the kettle on to boil without asking Mary Jo if she wanted a cup of tea.

going on in Erin's Glen, and there had been dramatic changes over the past couple of months. Not least, a change of boss. Father Gerard, the priest she had worked with for decades, was now gone, replaced by a younger man with some strange ideas. At least as far as Rosie was concerned. The many changes in Erin's Glen unsettled her, and she had much to think about on these walks. She had taken to coming through the woods now that the weather had improved and the days were longer. It was deeply unsettling to see news that even the fort itself, an ancient monument that had been in existence for millennia, was not immune to the effects of change and so-called progress. Before leaving the woods, she turned around and looked at the hill fort. The mound dominated the woods. The grassy banks were ringed by terraced walls and ramparts. The steep curve of the convex hill rose to a flat surface on which a majestic oak tree flourished. The locals called it 'The fairy ring,' and many believed that the little folk inhabited the mound's interior. Rosie pursed her lips and sighed. She intuitively sensed it would cause trouble.

Rosie returned from the woods along a country path that opened into a sparsely housed residential area. Her small, neat bungalow was at the end of the road on the way back towards town. Its tidy garden, floral curtains and freshly painted door welcomed her home.

As she put the key in the door and stepped inside, a tall figure loomed behind her, creating a shadow in the early morning sunlight. She felt a hand on her shoulder before she turned around.

'Good morning, Rosie.'

Chapter Three

Rosie's Rant

'Oh, dear God, don't creep up on me like that!' Rosie chided her longtime friend Mary Jo.

Mary Jo – or Sister Mary Joseph – was setting off for an early morning run. A Carmelite nun living locally, she worked as a Physical Education teacher at the local school. She was often out and about walking briskly, jogging or even swimming in the river that ran through Erin's Glen.

'Ah, Rosie, I'm sorry; I just wanted to catch you quickly to ask if you heard the news.'

Both women entered the hall of Rosie's bungalow; Rosie deftly got out of her coat and boots and undid Ziggy's collar as she answered. 'I saw a notice up in the forest about planning permission for an interpretation centre. What do you make of it?'

As usual, Rosie put the kettle on to boil without asking Mary Jo if she wanted a cup of tea.

Rosie stood with her back to the counter, facing Mary Jo, teaspoon held aloft as she warmed to her subject, 'Well, there's going to be stiff opposition, I can tell you, not least from that commune that has set up at the foot of the mountain.' Mary Jo was nodding her head in agreement as Rosie gave her opinion. 'And they will have trouble getting builders to work on such a place. You know as well as I do that superstition about the *Shee* is still alive and well.' Rosie referred to the fairies by their traditional Irish name. Rosie placed two cups onto their saucers and arranged the tea things. She continued, 'I know big burly men who have refused to work on building roads because the route disturbed a fairy fort. Sure, if you go up to the fort here, you will see people still leaving offerings. I've come across bits of food and small dishes of milk when I've been out walking Ziggy, especially at *Bealtaine* and *Shamhna*.' Rosie was referring to May Day and Halloween.

Mary Jo nodded her head in agreement. The plans were certainly contentious and would undoubtedly unsettle the locals.

The kettle hissed and whistled into life, and Rosie filled the substantial brown teapot with hot water and spooned in plenty of loose tea. She pulled on her handknitted angel tea cosy and sat down to enjoy the brew with her friend.

Mary Jo steered the conversation onto a more personal track. 'Anyway, how are you getting on with the new boss?' Mary Jo asked, referring to the new parish priest who had taken over from the old priest, Father Gerard, who had been relocated to another parish.

Rosie considered her words carefully. 'Well, he certainly has different ideas to Father Gerard, that's for sure. He's a bit too New Age for my liking.'

Mary Jo laughed heartily, 'What? Just because he has a ponytail and wears black jeans instead of the standard issue priest's get-up. Sure, he's just keeping up with the younger generation and staying current. I like him. Personally, I think we need a bit of a shake-up – fresh blood and all that.'

'Sure, you like everybody,' Rosie teased. 'And be careful what you wish for!'

It was true that Mary Jo looked compassionately at most people she met and tried to speak kindly of everyone. However, she was usually a good judge of character.

'Not everyone. Anyway, what do you mean by "New Age"? Mary Jo asked her friend to be more specific.

Rosie put her head to one side to think. At her feet, Ziggy also put his head to one side as if considering the same question. However, his eyes slid hopefully to the remains of a scone on Rosie's plate, abandoned as she considered her answer to Mary Jo's question.

After a moment or two, Rosie came up with some evidence to indicate the new priest, Father Asher Callaghan, was not as orthodox as she thought he should be.

Rosie put her cup down and began, 'Okay, he wants to start a Mindful Meditation group. I have no idea what that is, but it sounds weird to me. We don't do all that meditation stuff. Could you imagine it, me and Mrs Blaney sitting cross-legged chanting "Hum"?'

'You mean "Omn", Mary Jo corrected.

'Whatever, but you get my point.' Rosie continued.

Mary Jo argued gently, 'There's nothing wrong with a bit of meditation. The Desert Fathers themselves went off to isolated places to meditate and contemplate.'

Rosie blinked behind her glasses, seeing that this was not enough to convince her friend. Rosie carried on, 'Well, saying the Rosary has been good enough for me all these years, I'm not changing to new-fangled meditation now.'

Mary Jo nodded sympathetically. She did not totally agree with her friend, but she knew that Rosie was on a roll, so she didn't interrupt.

'And another thing, he's all into being "green" and not in the Irish sense. He's too "eco", if you know what I mean. He's keeping a compost bin in the kitchen and expects me to tip it out onto a heap in the garden, dirty thing.' Rosie tutted, 'He's told me not to bring in any plastic bags and keeps lecturing me about looking after the environment; that's like those hippies up the hill. Not like a good Catholic priest at all. It's a disgrace.' Rosie paused just long enough to take a breath. 'And he's taken in a stray cat, too. I can't tell you the havoc it's caused, especially if I bring Ziggy to work with me.'

When Mary Jo was confident that Rosie had come to the end of her rant against Father Asher Callaghan for now, she asked quietly, 'So was St Francis "New Age" in your opinion?'

'St Francis?' Rosie queried.

'Well, he talked about "Sister Moon and Brother Sun" didn't he?' Mary Jo reminded the parish secretary that her boss was in step with one of the church's most beloved saints.

'Well, I suppose so....' Rosie agreed grudgingly.

Mary Jo realised, from recent experience, that Rosie would come up with more reasons to feel uneasy about the new priest, so she decided to change the subject quickly.

'Will you be going to the craft group on Wednesday evening?' Mary Jo knew that Rosie enjoyed this get-together at a local bookshop and café in town, which was usually once a week on a Wednesday evening.

At last, Rosie was off her current pet topic and moved on to muse on how the group had grown since it started a few months earlier. She took a quick gulp of tea and smiled, 'Oh yes, indeed, I will. We need to get the production line going for the May Day celebrations. We've got quite a few projects on the go, and sure, it's great to catch up with everyone and share a bit of craic. Right, well, I'll have to throw you out now; I've got to get to the hairdressers in a bit.'

Mary Jo stood up, 'Great. I'll get off for this jog now anyway. If I don't see you over the weekend, I'll catch up with you at the craft group.' Mary Jo hugged her friend and trotted briskly out the door. Dressed in a brown tracksuit and trainers, she jogged off up the road towards the forest, which provided a broad ring of deep foliage around the mound that rose in the middle.

Heavy clouds now obscured the early morning sunshine, and a gloom had descended over Erin's Glen. The sky looked grey and sombre. Many trees still had bare branches and stood in stark outlines against the leaden clouds. Mary Jo jogged steadily at a slower pace than usual. The sudden heaviness of the day weighed down on her. She carried along a dirt path through the wooded area. Over the winter, she had not been up to the hill fort due to the slippery mud and lack of light on dark winter mornings and evenings. So, now Mary Jo enjoyed tuning into the birdsong. Such simple natural delights of spring lifted her mood.

As she approached the hill fort, the birdsong seemed to stop abruptly. An eerie silence descended. Mary Jo stopped in her tracks and looked at the highest point on the hill. The tree at the top was silhouetted against the grey sky. She spotted a figure under it. Mary Jo was intrigued and stood perplexed. Something very odd was happening in Erin's Glen, and it all seemed to focus on the fairy ring.

Chapter Four

Time for Tea

Saturday mornings were always busy in the little café attached to Reid and Wright's Bookshop and Stationers. On an impulse, Mary Jo decided to go in and have a quick cup of tea after her jog around the town and up the hill. There was no point in risking dehydration.

As always, seeing the pastel-coloured frontage of the bookshop come teashop lifted her spirits. The café was an intoxicating combination of strong tea, books, people to chat with, and a tasty bite to eat. It was a mix that the sociable Mary Jo could not resist. After her unsettling encounter on the hill fort, she longed for the cosy familiarity of the welcoming establishment run by her friends, Marie and Deirdre.

She kept a five-punt note in her pocket to pay for her treat. Even religious sisters are allowed a little indulgence now and then, she reminded herself as she pushed open the door. Before the nun stepped into the shop, she glanced up at a weak ray of sunshine that was starting to peek through the clouds. The day was picking up.

The bell chimed to herald her arrival, and she was met with a hubbub of conversation punctuated by some laughter. Marie was standing at a table talking to Kay Byrne, one of their customers. Kay was a teacher at the school where Mary Jo worked. Mary Jo joined them at the small round table covered in a blue checked tablecloth.

Deirdre was serving at the stationary shop counter. A small, slim woman was paying for a fountain pen and ink. She smiled shyly at the nun, glancing at her from under long, curly eyelashes.

Deirdre waved over at the nun. 'Good morning, Sister! Your usual then?' She enquired as she slung a tea towel over her shoulder.

Mary Jo nodded as she sat down opposite her colleague and friend Kay.

Kay smiled, 'Oh, it's lovely to get to the weekend. What a week it's been! I'm exhausted!'

'I see you are getting the girls ready for the Irish dancing competition in May. You've got your work cut out for you there.' Mary Jo giggled. She had seen the recent cohort of Irish dancing hopefuls and didn't expect any of them to be invited onto the *Riverdance* troupe any time soon.

Kay pulled a face, 'Tell me about it. I've seen more graceful elephants! Honest to God, I was worried about the stage caving in under those girls of mine, stomping up and down!'

'Ah, you'll get them sorted in no time. You do it every year.' Mary Jo smiled, trying to encourage the dance and drama teacher.

'Thanks for your vote of confidence, Mary Jo.' Kay Byrne returned to her soda bread, toasted and dripping with butter.

The smell of freshly baked bread wafted out of the kitchen, and Mary Jo's stomach began to rumble. Although she had already imbibed a few cups of tea, she hadn't eaten that day, and she was looking forward to her Saturday morning special: a large mug of tea with a buttered potato farl and a poached egg.

Marie and Deirdre were now both in the small kitchen, getting orders together and murmuring to each other. *Radio Erin* was on in the background. The Saturday morning show was dedicated to traditional Irish music. Mary Jo took a moment to savour the aroma of baked goodies. The soft hum of conversation surrounded her, and she felt the gentle warmth of the sunlight coming in through the lace curtains at the window.

Mary Jo looked around at her fellow customers, waving and smiling at familiar locals as she took in the scene. Mrs Blaney, the owner of the local B&B, was in the corner, holding court with Mrs Kirkpatrick from the post office.

Mary Jo let the warmth and familiarity wash over her, tired from her busy week at work and taking care of the older sisters at Riverside House, where she lived. Just as Mary Jo was being lulled into a hypnotic state, the bell over the door jingled loudly, and Fiona Fitzgerald swept in. Before the dramatic Fiona reached the counter, she called out, 'Please be a darling and do me a large green tea to go,' some locals looked askance at the tall, elegant lady dressed in a black jumpsuit and long dark grey blazer.

'Fiona held the door open and called back to the taxi driver, 'I'll just be two ticks.'. The driver kept the engine running as he waited.

Much to the relief of the customers inside, Fiona let the door close behind her as she approached the counter, hunting in her bag for her purse.

Deirdre came out of the kitchen with Fiona's tea in a large paper cup with a plastic lid.

'There you go, Fiona, off to the airport on your travels again?' Deirdre asked cheerfully.

'Oh, my dear, you don't know the half of it!' Fiona spoke in a low-pitched, musical tone. Her drama training at the Lyric Theatre served her well in her public speaking role in the European Parliament. 'It's no holiday, I can assure you. I've got lunch with Glynis – Glynis Kinnock, we are working on addressing a range of women's issues, then I'll have tea with Pat – you have seen him on the news, Pat Cox, President of the E.C – The European Community,' Fiona paused, allowing this to sink in. Deirdre blinked. Fiona's name-dropping was lost on her.

Fiona's driver tooted the horn. She glanced around and sighed; not finished yet, she continued, 'Then, there will be back-to-back meetings and conferences, and I'll speak on funding for the regeneration of rural Ireland. You can rest assured I will fully represent all your interests.' Fiona swept her gaze around the café, smiling with her arm outstretched towards her not-so-adoring public.

Tall, with glossy black hair in a shoulder-length bouffant style, Fiona oozed sophistication and glamour, or so she liked to think. In truth, many of the locals giggled at her dramatic style and pulled faces at her penchant for name-dropping. 'Sorry, dear, I need to rush. Bye.' Fiona gave a royal wave to all those assembled and, with a whiff of Channel No. 5 in her wake, whisked off out the door and slid onto the back seat of the taxi waiting by the kerbside.

'Count yourself honoured, Deirdre, being graced by the local MEP no less!' Mrs Blaney called over from her table in the corner. She had been watching Fiona's little speech with amused interest, her merry eyes darting about under her high-arched eyebrows. 'Well, I'm glad I didn't miss it, but I need to make a move now, ladies,' Mrs Blaney's face took on a determined expression as she addressed the trio assembled at her table. 'I'm paying.'

'No, you are not!' Her friends called out in unison.

'I am indeed.' Mrs Blaney looked stony-faced. She bolted to the counter and got there first, with her friends hot on her heels.

Deirdre and Marie were accustomed to this show every week. When they chatted at home upstairs about the workday, they would bet with each other on who would win the battle to pay next time.

This morning, Mrs Blaney succeeded. Despite hot protests from her companions, she was the quickest off the draw and got the purse out first.

'Right, now I'm off to get my hair done at Trish's. See you all soon!' Mrs Blaney waved to all the customers and was so busy looking behind her that she nearly got knocked over by the door opening abruptly.

She stepped back and blinked at the latest arrival. The man of mystery from down the road had decided to grace the teashop that morning. Mary Jo wondered what he would have to say for himself.

Chapter Five

Hot News

Mrs Blaney sped along the high street known to the locals of Erin's Glen as Rainbow Row. This was due to the bright pastel shades of most of the shops and businesses along the street. It was an attractive assortment of traditional buildings of varying heights and widths. The rainbow colours brightened up even the dreariest of winter days; today, Rainbow Row looked particularly charming.

The high street was cheerful but quiet. Until recently, Saturday mornings were usually the busiest time of the week in Erin's Glen. But a large shopping centre had been built in Rocksheelan a few miles away, and with the lure of ample, free parking and an array of large, smart new shops to choose from, many of the locals, especially the younger crowd, chose to go there for their weekly shopping expedition.

However, Mrs Blaney had no time to admire the charms of her local town or worry about the threats of progress. She hurried along as if on a mission to O'Hara's Hair and Beauty Salon, run by the chatty and all-knowing Trish O'Hara. As the local guest house owner, Mrs Blaney took it upon herself to stay informed about local events, and her once-a-week trip to the hairdressers was a great source of information.

Rosie was already ensconced in a highbacked salon chair, having her hair combed and sprayed with hairspray as Mrs Blaney entered the usually busy salon. It, too, was quiet this morning; the only sound was the soft murmur of the radio in the kitchen at the back. Rosie and Trish were speaking together in hushed whispers; Trish bent down to Rosie's ear in conversation. She listened carefully and looked at Rosie in the mirror as she combed her hair. Trish immediately bolted upright as Mrs Blaney entered.

'Ach, hello there, Mrs B!' Trish called out.' We were only talking about you.' Trish grinned innocently, a glint in her eye.

Mrs Blaney's eyes darted between the two women, trying to determine whether this was a good thing. She didn't take the bait and instead sat on a soft chair in the waiting area with a magazine she had no intention of reading.

'Not much doin' in here today, Trish. How's business?' the latest customer to the salon looked around her meaningfully.

'We were saying the same, Mrs Blaney. I don't suppose *you've* had many guests staying with you lately?' Rosie was referring to Mrs Blaney's B&B down the road.

'Well, I'm glad of the rest, to be honest.' Mrs Blaney sniffed.

Rosie and Trish exchanged glances.

Rosie couldn't resist doing a bit of stirring, 'Ach, sure, now everyone is feeling the pinch, aren't they? I love the peace here in Erin's Glen, but we're not on the tourist map at all, and we get overlooked, don't we? Tourist accommodation just isn't needed here much.' Rosie smiled over at Mrs Blaney, who had her eyes fixed on an *Avon* catalogue in her hands, seeming to ignore Rosie's latest comment.

Mrs Blaney, unwilling to share details of her business difficulties, changed the subject yet again, 'I see that Fiona Fitzgerald is off on her jollies again, back to Brussels.' Rosie and Trish looked at her, waiting for more information. 'I don't know how she can afford it. She's got her mother at home to look after, and I've heard she has to pay a nurse to look after her when she goes away. I know that the European Community covers travelling expenses, but I bet even they don't pay to have her mother looked after.' Mrs Blaney blinked expectantly at her companions.

These insights didn't have much of an impression on the other two women. Rosie didn't respond, and Trish carried on combing Rosie's hair, unperturbed. Determined to get a reaction, the local B&B owner carried on,' *I* think it's a disgrace the way she leaves her poor mother to be looked after by *strangers*.'

Rosie cleared her throat and said loudly and pointedly, 'I'll be off now, Trish; I need to get going.'

Mrs Blaney, clearly irritated that her opinions elicited such little interest, sniffed again and flicked through the magazine's pages. With her eyes fixed on her reading material, she called out, 'I'll have tea, milk and two sugars when you're ready, Trish.'

Trish grinned with little warmth and responded flatly, 'Of course, Mrs B. No worries.'

Rosie rolled her eyes and paid Trish, ensuring she gave her a good tip. She was alarmed to see that business at the hairdressers was so quiet this morning.

Mrs Blaney raised a hand to bid an unenthusiastic farewell to Rosie, keeping her eyes fixed on the small catalogue in her lap.

'Cheerio ladies,' Rosie called brightly.

'Bye, Rosie, and thanks.' Trish waved enthusiastically to her customer and friend and then turned to deal with Mrs Blaney. 'Right then, let's get you that tea.'

Trish went to the kitchen at the back of the shop and switched on the radio. Partly to discourage the nosey B&B owner from further enquiries about her business and partly to listen to the midday news bulletin. Trish was aware that her customers expected her to be a font of knowledge and information on local events, so she was keen to tune in regularly and keep up with the local news.

A traditional music show was coming to an end, and Trish hummed along with a jaunty tune about fairies playing the pipes. As it finished, the DJ came on.

'Well, there you have it. That's the show wrapped up for today. And on the subject of the fairy folk, we've just had news that an ancient monument known as the fairy ring in the small town of Erin's Glen has become the subject of controversy. Planning permission has been sought to build an interpretation centre on the fort. SB Builders, a local firm, is generally believed to be handling the project. Stay tuned for the news coming up. We will have an interview with Gerry Macauley, the Erin's Glen councillor.'

Trish switched the radio up as she re-entered the salon, a steaming mug of tea in her hand.

'Let's hear what he's got to say for himself.' Trish swathed her customer in a black hairdressing cape as they both listened to the news, waiting for the interview with the man who had grown up in Erin's Glen and was now representing their interests. After the usual round-up of international headlines and national news, the program switched to local issues and aired the promised interview.

'Thank you for coming in to talk to us this morning, Mr Macauley. We realise how busy you are. Now tell us what you think of this application and how it will affect the residents of Erin's Glen.'

Gerry Macauley spoke in smooth, oily tones, well used to placating irate residents and confrontational interviewers.

'Well, firstly, thank you for inviting me onto the show today. It's always a pleasure to visit the studios here at *Radio Erin*. I appreciate that many of the listeners today will have their own steadfast opinions about the proposal, but rest assured, I take my job of representing the different interests and opinions expressed by the members of my constituency very seriously. I do not take the responsibility bestowed on me lightly, and I am keen that all aspects of this case are thoroughly considered and all angles examined.'

'Right, okay, thanks for that, Mr Macauley. But what do *you* think about the proposal?

'Well, as I said, I am keen to present the interests of all involved in the best possible light when I vote on this issue in our chamber next week. We are still garnering opinions and thoughts on this matter, and I am keen to hear everyone's views.'

'Thanks, Mr Macauley.'

The interviewer's exasperation became apparent, but he continued: 'Can you tell me if you think the interpretation centre should be built? What is *your* opinion on the matter, and which side will you support?'

'Well now,' Gerry Macauley snorted a small laugh. 'I must put my own opinions on the matter to one side and represent the interests of my constituents. What I will say is that Erin's Glen is not on the tourist map and has suffered dreadfully from being overlooked in this way. Businesses are closing, and just a few months ago, a public house in the town, The Thatch, closed its doors for the last time. The town is struggling. We live in changing times and must keep up with the pace of change.'

'So, I would understand from your comments today that you support the centre's construction?'

'I am simply commenting on the economic downturn the town has suffered. It is a fact that we need to take action to stem the tide of oblivion that Erin's Glen is facing.'

'Now, Mr Macauley, what would you say to people concerned about the environmental impact?'

'I am sure that the centre will be built in a way that respects the environment. I have no doubts about that.'

'I see. And lastly, Mr Macauley, how would you allay the fears of some of Erin's Glens residents concerned about disturbing the little people?'

Gerry Macauley let out a loud laugh and sighed.

'Ah, for goodness' sake, this is 1990, not the Dark Ages. We've moved on from all that superstitious nonsense, surely! I'm concerned about creating jobs and opportunities for our young people, not perpetuating fairy tales and superstitions. Let's focus on the facts; the numbers add up. I'm working closely with our MEP, Ms Fiona Fitzgerald, and we are very hopeful of securing European Community funding for the project. It's a hugely exciting opportunity that will create dozens of jobs in construction and hospitality. It's the best thing to hit Erin's Glen in decades.'

The interview was cut at this, and the newscaster made no further comment.

Mrs Blaney looked at Trish with wide eyes below her high-arched eyebrows. 'No good will come of this. You can mark my words. That young idiot will rue the day he set himself up against the wee people.

They don't like to be disturbed no matter how many jobs it might bring.'

Trish was not a fan of this inquisitive customer. In the past, Mrs Blaney had put her nose in where it was not wanted, as far as Trish was concerned. But even Trish had to concede and agree with Mrs Blaney. Despite what the councillor said, disturbing the ancient fort for economic progress would not be popular with the locals. Even in 1990, the belief that the *Shee* were powerful beings who would wreak revenge on anyone who disturbed them was prevalent. Begrudgingly, Trish nodded in agreement with her opinionated client.

'Now, Mrs B, is it the usual you want today, or do you want a change of look?' Trish smiled mischievously and switched on the hair clippers as she approached Mrs B playfully. 'I could buzz you all over like that girl Sinead O'Connor. Sure, it's all the rage. What d'ya say?'

'Ach away on with you! You're a right cod,' Mrs Blaney swiped at her cheeky hairdresser, chiding her gently for trying to be the comic.

A few miles away, Fiona Fitzgerald and her taxi driver were also listening to the interview on the radio as she continued her journey to the airport. The driver chose to keep a diplomatic silence on the matter. Fiona listened with a slight smile on her face. Her silver Parker pen held aloft as she paused to listen. Her free hand pushed a strand of black hair behind her ear. She had been busy putting the finishing touches to her application for the funding Gerry Macauley was referring to, feeling confident she could secure it. When the interview finished, she returned to her paperwork with assured satisfaction that all would be well.

Unlike Fiona, many people in Erin's Glen were unhappy with what they heard that morning on the radio – and they weren't all little.

Chapter Six

Quinn's Curiosities

Cornelius Quinn took a seat in a quiet corner at the back of the teashop. He was a dapper man in his sixties with a silver goatee beard, and he carried a cane more as an affectation than a necessity. Although he was a private man and a mystery to many locals, he was a familiar figure. His antique shop further along Rainbow Row had been in Erin's Glen for at least a decade, but only a few people knew much about the man himself. Of course, his cousin, Connell Quinn, ran the local supermarket, Super-Quinn, so his family connection to Erin's Glen was no mystery. Only a few people questioned his presence in the town.

The news that was seeping across the consciousness of the locals that morning had also gripped Cornelius's interest. He was curious about how the people of the town were receiving it, hence his uncommon visit to the teashop. He thought he'd put a few feelers out and see how people reacted.

However, Cornelius decided to sit quietly and keep his ears open rather than get involved in direct conversations.

'Good morning,' Marie called over. She was keen to welcome all customers, especially infrequent ones, and smiled warmly at the older gentleman in the silk waistcoat and well-pressed trousers. Marie had already visited his antique shop, and they had shared a few words about Erin's Glen and its fascinating history.

Cornelius waved away her offer of a menu and gave her a faint smile: 'Good morning, Marie. I would like a pot of Earl Grey tea with lemon and a slice of wholemeal toast with Seville marmalade. No butter. Thank you.'

Marie took his order and distracted by a more loquacious customer, stopped to chat on her way back to the small kitchen where Deirdre was preparing the orders.

Cornelius, in no rush, made himself comfortable. He had brought a publication with him to read while he eavesdropped on the hubbub of conversation that swirled around him. He shook out his copy of *IT for Antiques*, pushed his small wire-rimmed glasses back up his slightly hooked nose and raised his head a fraction to focus on the print before him.

'Ah, IT – Information Technology, I'm getting into some of that myself.'

Cornelius peered up to see who was speaking.

Rosie had just come in for a quick cup of tea and a light snack before heading home from the hairdresser. In truth, she also wanted to gauge the impact of the big news about the proposed tourist centre, so she decided to pop into the café to assess the local feeling about the developments.

'Indeed? Good morning, Rosie.' Cornelius greeted his fellow customer, and without invitation, Rosie sat down on the seat opposite the antique shop owner.

'Yes, I did a course a while back with a lovely lad from the IT training team at the Diocese.' Rosie was referring to a session she had as Parish Secretary.

Cornelius nodded and smiled politely.

'Oh yes, he was great, ever so patient. I'm still unsure about using the computer; we just covered the basics, but he explained a lot about using Windows and Word. I've got a course coming up on bed sheets, but I haven't got a clue.'

'Spreadsheets', Cornelius corrected the technophobe.

'That's it – spreadsheets!' Rosie rolled her eyes and smiled, then asked, 'What are they, anyway?'

Cornelius hesitated for a second. He knew he might regret what he said next, but on quick reflection, he realised that having Rosie on board might turn out to be very useful.

'Well, Rosie, I think the best thing to do would be for you to pop into my shop when you have a moment, and I can show you exactly what they are and what they do on my machine.'

Rosie clapped her hands gleefully, and the other customers glanced over at the couple at the table, wondering what the good news was. 'Ah, Mr Quinn, that's just grand. Oh, I'd really appreciate that. I'm not very good with computers, and all this new-fangled business using IT worries me. You're an absolute angel.'

'Call me Cornelius.'

'Ah, right, so' Rosie looked a bit doubtful. She appreciated his offer to explain the mysteries of spreadsheets, but she was not totally comfortable with this small, quiet man with the pretentious name.

Cornelius returned his gaze to his magazine, and Rosie sat quietly, her hands folded in her lap, looking around her. Although a chatty, friendly creature, Rosie was quite content to people-watch, and over the years, she had learned that much was to be gained from just sitting and watching on the sidelines.

'Your usual Rosie?' Marie called over as she was preparing the Earl Grey for Cornelius.

'Thanks, Marie. Yes, you know me, a creature of habit, just the same. Thanks, Marie.' Rosie confirmed her favourite order of a large fruit scone and a pot of tea for two, which she usually managed to get through singlehandedly.

Cornelius had retreated behind his IT magazine. The teashop had emptied now, and Rosie sat blinking, looking at the cover of the IT magazine Cornelius was scanning with interest.

Rosie cleared her throat. Cornelius glanced over the top of his magazine and politely folded it as he accepted his Earl Grey tea. Rosie watched with gentle amusement as he shook out his napkin, placed it carefully across his lap, and then arranged his toast and a small dish of marmalade on the table before him.'

'So, what type of computer do you have then?' Rosie was keen to break the silence by pursuing a topic of apparent interest to her companion.

Cornelius responded, 'I have an IBM PS/2 PC with a DOS operating system and Intel 286 processor – with a monochrome monitor.'

'Ah, that's grand.' Rosie nodded. Her smile froze on her face as her heart sank. She realised she had no idea what he was talking about.

Luckily, just then, her tea and scone arrived, and Rosie and Cornelius focused on their food and beverages.

Rosie decided to change the subject to one she was more knowledgeable about, 'I see you like a drop of the old Earl Grey then?' she nodded at the small pot in front of him.

'Yes, indeed,' Cornelius dapped delicately at his lips. 'This is an acceptable blend, but I think my true preference is for Lady Grey tea, which has a much more subtle taste.'

'Ah, that's lovely. I like Punjana Tea myself. At a push, I'd have PG Tips. Nothing beats a good cup of tea,' Rosie enthused as she poured herself a second cup.

Rosie watched Cornelius finish his toast and drained the last few drops of tea from his little cup – he always had a small cup and saucer.

She realised she knew little about this neat, private man who ran the local antique shop. Just why had he moved back to Erin's Glen after decades away? Where exactly had he been, and what had he been doing?

Rosie decided to visit him in his shop and learn more. His offer to unveil the mysteries of spreadsheets on his computer might help her unravel a few more mysteries of a more personal nature.

She made a mental note to visit his shop, Quinn's Curiosities, sooner rather than later.

Chapter Seven

Newsround

Later that evening, just as the sun was getting lower in the sky and the day's warmth was cooling off, Rosie settled down in front of the television. Her dinner was on a tray, and Ziggy was at her feet, ever hopeful of a stray morsel coming his way. Her mother had always insisted that they ate at the table, and despite her advanced years, Rosie still felt slightly naughty eating her food in this casual way in front of the television.

She had been bustling about in her kitchen all afternoon, cooking up some meals for the next few days when she would be out at work. She favoured hearty stews and soups and always enjoyed a roast dinner on a Sunday. Today, she was also busy baking a cake to take to the craft group on Wednesday evening at the bookshop. Deirdre from the bookshop-come-café was a great baker. However, Rosie wanted to give her a break from the responsibility of providing the treats and offered to bake a lemon drizzle cake, her personal favourite.

On a recent trip to a department store in Rocksheelan, Rosie bought a cupcake maker. She decided that today was the day to try it. Instead of a slab cake, she would make lemon cupcakes with lemon-frosted icing on top. She could picture them in her mind, glistening and irresistible. She began mixing, whisking, and studying the instructions for her new gadget.

The spring sunshine had streamed in through the south-facing kitchen window all afternoon, and Rosie's wispy grey hair had become a bedraggled halo around her shiny face, flushed from her exertions and the warm sunshine. So now, as she sat down at last to enjoy her dinner, she sighed deeply, grateful to be off her feet.

'Right now, let's see what's been happening today.' Ziggy looked at her expectantly, his head to one side as he considered what she said. The late afternoon Sunday drama ended, and a brief local news bulletin was about to begin.

After the usual introductions, footage from Erin's Glen flashed up on the screen. A news reporter commented on what had been happening in the town that day: 'This afternoon, there was a demonstration on the main road in Erin's Glen. A small group of New Age travellers from the camp close to the woods at the foot of the mountain in Erin's Glen were out protesting against the construction of a new attraction in the small town.'

The footage showed the group of protestors. They were not at all like the usual people around Erin's Glen. Men with long hair and multi-coloured trousers held up placards. A woman wearing what Rosie thought looked like a sack and with bare feet stood next to him. The footage then switched to the woods at Erin's Glen. The camera panned around the forest as the commentator explained how the area provided valuable green space for local ramblers and dog walkers. Gerry Macauley, the regional councillor, then came into view. He was standing with his back to the camera and appeared to be looking at the woods thoughtfully.

'Mr Macauley.' The news reporter pushed a microphone with a large fuzzy head in Gerry Macauley's direction. Gerry Macauley swung around to face the camera, grinning from ear to ear.

'Mr Macauley, you are the local councillor for the area; how do you feel about the proposed building of the Tourist Interpretation Centre at Erin's Glen Woods?'

Gerry Macauley smiled briefly at the news reporter and looking straight into the camera with studied sincerity, began his speech:

'Thank you for coming out today to talk to me. I am, of course, very concerned that all of our residents are fully informed about decisions affecting an area of natural beauty on their doorstep. I am very aware of the concerns some people might have. I have listened to a broad selection of the electorate in Erin's Glen, and I can assure you.' Gerry Macauley hesitated here just for a second, looking into the camera with intensity, ' I can assure you that the vast majority of *established residents* in our lovely town are in support of this project that will create jobs and put Erin's Glen on the map––'

Rosie tuned out at this point, realising that Gerry Macauley was going to repeat his usual patter. She was also distracted by a figure in the background who had strolled into view behind Gerry Macauley. The dishevelled-looking man sat down on a low wall behind the councillor. He watched the exchange between the reporter and the councillor like a tennis match, peering at their faces from one to the other. Rosie leaned closer to the television to see who it was: a middle-aged man with shaggy dark hair and a stubbly chin. He grinned with an uncertain, gap-toothed smile, his eyes darting around, trying to make sense of what was going on. He was wearing a tee shirt with a slogan that said 'Disco Fever.' It looked like a scruffy hand-me-down. Rosie was trying to place the familiar face. She always remembered a face, but sometimes names could take a while to recall. After a moment, she tuned back into the conversation between the reporter and Gerry.

The reporter was questioning Gerry, 'What about the people who were out protesting this afternoon? Not all residents of Erin's Glen are happy about this development.' The reporter pressed Gerry Macauley, who had kept his expression of grave concern. Gerry listened carefully with a furrowed brow.

When the reporter had finished asking his question, Gerry's face creased into a condescending smile. Then, with a sigh, he continued, 'Ah, now I said *"established residents"* I think the people you'll be referring to are the transient group we have up the hill, by the foot of the mountain. I can assure the concerned tax-paying citizens of Erin's Glen that this group, which has been causing such an inconvenience in the town, will be moved on as soon as possible. These travellers you are talking about have moved into Erin's Glen to cause trouble. I believe they were out on the roads, causing a disturbance this morning. This will not be tolerated. I am working with the authorities to ensure they are removed as soon as possible.'

The reporter hesitated for a second, then, conscious of the time pressure, had to wrap up the interview as time was limited for this Sunday bulletin.

'Thank you, Mr Macauley. This is Barry Cullen from Erin's Glen, now back to the studio.'

The news then switched to the events that Rosie was sure would be of much more interest to those in other local villages and towns – the sports results and round-up from the weekend.

Rosie sat thoughtfully, eating her dinner and thinking over her impressions from that day. It niggled her that she couldn't recall the name of the dark-haired man in the background during the interview.

'Who *is* that?'

Ziggy looked at Rosie, his large honey eyes fixed on her face, hoping he would be allowed to finish the rest of her roast chicken, which was now cold on her plate.

Just then, the phone rang.

Rosie pushed her tray table away and padded out to the hallway, where the phone was found on a small table with a seat attached. Rosie picked up the phone. It was her friend Mary Jo.

'Have you had your tea, Rosie?' Mary Jo asked anxiously.

'I have indeed. How are you doing yourself?' Rosie asked her friend. Now, before we get talking, please help me with something. Have you been watching the news?' When Mary Jo confirmed that she had, Rosie asked if she had recognised the man in the background.

'Ach, yes, sure, that's wee Toddy.'

'Wee Toddy?' Rosie queried, trying to place him.

'Yes, sure, he lives in that ramshackle cottage on the edge of the woods. He's always standing by the gate, watching what's happening.'

'Ah, of course...' The light of recognition dawned on Rosie as she continued, 'I remember now, he had scarlet fever as a child. He was in and out of the hospital, a very sickly wee boy, never at school much.'

'Yes, that's right,' Mary Jo carried on, 'He's never had a job as such, but he lives in that cottage that belonged to his parents and gets by with a bit of poaching and doing odd jobs around the town. Although I hardly ever see him around the town, to be fair. He's a harmless critter, for sure. Anyway, I rang to chat about all this going on. I'm worried about what all this talk about tearing up the woods might lead to.'

Rosie stayed quiet while her friend gathered her thoughts. After a few moments, Rosie asked, 'Surely you're not worried about the fairies?'

Mary Jo laughed heartily. No, I am more worried about human folk and what they might get up to. You know better than me that plenty of people in this town have secrets to hide. All this talk about digging up the old ground and people getting all fired up about it doesn't bode well.'

'Yes, I know what you mean,' Rosie agreed. 'So, is there anything specifically on your mind, Mary Jo?'

The nun sighed.

'Well, I was in the woods out for a run yesterday, and I saw something that puzzled me at the time; I couldn't understand what I was looking at. But something occurred to me today, so I wanted to ring and discuss it with you to see what you make of it.'

Mary Jo went on to share what she had seen. As Rosie listened, her eyes grew large behind her thick spectacles.

Chapter Eight

An Elemental Discovery

The following day, it was still dark when Mary Jo stepped outside the door of Riverside House, where she lived with the other nuns. Her usual morning routine was to go for a brisk jog before breakfast, and today was no exception. She zipped up her thick tracksuit top against the spring morning chill and set off down the street with a quick trot to warm up. As a Physical Education teacher, she felt it was her duty to keep fit, and these early morning runs gave her time to think and sometimes to pray, too. As a longtime resident of Erin's Glen, she was unsettled by all the talk of the proposed new development. Knowing human nature, she was more disturbed by the effect such changes might have on the people in her hometown than any of the local superstitions about the little folk. Although not shy about speaking up, she disliked controversy and was upset by some of the townsfolk's passionate responses for and against the proposal to build on the sacred spot.

The town was quiet, and as she pondered the issues connected with the hill fort, she decided to head up there this morning. A while back, she had seen Cornelious Quinn up there. One of her colleagues informed her that he was often seen out with his metal detector. She had seen him herself, scanning the top of the hill, and she vaguely wondered if he would be up there this morning. A few streaks of daylight spread out into the inky morning darkness, and she reckoned that the sun would just be rising as she reached the fort.

Mary Jo could hear the soft thud of her trainers on the pavement, and the steady rhythm lulled her into a meditative state. She felt calmed by the familiar sound of her steps as she jogged along. The unease she had woken up with began to lift. As she neared the outskirts of the small town, she could see the silhouette of the hill fort clearly defined against the morning sky. The distinctive oak stood regally on the very top of the hill and created a landmark in the locality. She wondered idly if the tree would be saved, and as she had this thought, she felt a sense of profound loss and regret about the possibility of it being chopped down to make way for a new building.

As she looked up, she was struck by the transformative beauty of the scene as the sun rose behind the hill fort. The light transfigured the scene around the mound and illuminated the land and the fields around it, glowing emerald in the sun's early rays as it crept up behind the hill. The scene's natural beauty struck Mary Jo, and she hoped it would remain untouched for generations to come.

As Mary Jo entered the woodland, she noticed the crisp dew that seemed to hang in the air between the trees. A soft mist swirled about the forest floor; the vapour caught the sun's rays here and there, and its jewel-like hues added an ethereal feel to the early morning scene. Mary

Jo slowed down as she entered the woodland, conscious of tree roots she might trip over.

She stopped abruptly. Mary Jo, suddenly alert, listened carefully; she thought she had heard a twig crack in her wake. Was someone following her? She quickly swung around. A branch snapped back a few paces behind her. Not given to flights of fancy, the nun shrugged it off; it was probably a squirrel or a rabbit. She smiled at her silly imaginings and tried to march through the forest, focusing on the scene's beauty.

The mist was clearing now, and she was mesmerised by the interplay of light and shadow created by the sun filtered through the budding spring leaves on the skeletal trees. Bright patches of spring wildflowers were illuminated in the early sunshine, and bursts of purple and yellow flowers clustered around the trees. Mary Jo breathed in the refreshing scent of bluebells, hyacinths and daffodils. The harmonious sound of songbirds echoed through the trees, creating a background soundtrack to the sound of Mary Jo's feet shuffling through the leaves.

Suddenly, the bird song stopped. The wind picked up and rustled through the trees. The air took on a chill, and Mary Jo was conscious of the sound of her own heavy breathing. She stood stock still, every nerve and fibre of her being vigilant. She had a sense that something was not right and moved forward cautiously. As she came to the border of the densest part of the wood, she felt a sense of relief, but her relief was short-lived. Looking up towards the top of the hill, she saw an unfamiliar shape on the mound.

She paused, took a breath, and sprinted up quickly. Moving closer, she stopped again to take in what she saw. She moved slowly, keeping her eyes fixed on the strange image ahead. When she registered what it was, she blessed herself and took a deep breath, her heart beating hard and the sound of blood rushing in her ears.

The nun took a few seconds to collect herself and pray. She asked for strength and courage and moved forward with a look of resolve. Mary Jo took one last long stride and looked down at the object that had attracted her attention. Before she looked any closer, she turned around and scanned the woodland around her. The wind had settled, and the trees stood still. Steely grey clouds now moving across the sky, obliterating the early morning sunlight. A dark shadow seemed to pass over the woodland and hilltop, and an eerie sense of calm descended.

Mary Jo crouched down to look closer, perplexed by the effort someone had put into it. Her concerned eyes scanned the figure. The open eyes with their blank stare, ashen face and fixed expression indicated that all life had left this person. She brushed the face briefly with her fingertips – it was icy-cold to the touch. It appeared as if the corpse had been laid out ceremonially. A white sheet had been draped over the body, but the face was left uncovered. Mary Jo could see the shape of the arms crossed over the chest beneath the sheet. A sprig of mistletoe was placed on top where the hands appeared to be folded serenely. A small bowl of water had been placed to the left of the head and a pile of stones to the right. Mary Jo looked down at the feet – some feathers to the left and a small tealight candle by the right foot. The wind had extinguished the candle.

She backed away slowly, chilled to the bone by her eerie discovery. As soon as she got to the edge of the hilltop, she leapt down towards the woodland, sprinting quickly back to the town to raise the alarm. All concern about tripping over tree roots was gone, replaced by an almost primal fear: she felt the need to escape this death scene and reconnect with the living. She ran back through the forest at top speed, branches whipping back at her as she pushed through swiftly, gulping deep breaths of air as she moved. Suddenly, the rain clouds burst open, and she was soaked by the time she returned to Riverside House.

She almost fell into the hall of her home and grabbed the phone, dialling 999. 'Sergeant Kennedy, it's Mary Jo here. I've just found a body up on the hill fort. You need to get up there right away.'

Chapter Nine

A Dark Morning

That same morning, on impulse, an unwitting Rosie took Ziggy for a quick trot up towards the fairy ring. She had felt an odd compulsion to go up there. She had dressed quickly in the half-light. On these cold mornings, she was particularly glad of her tea machine. She had been dubious to begin with and had a few disasters with using the machine. But she had persevered and now had it set to make a welcome cup of tea at 6.30 am. The hissing and sloshing the machine made was enough of an alarm to wake her up in plenty of time to take Ziggy for a walk before work. She sat up in bed for a few minutes, enjoying the warmth of the tea and watching the first strands of light filter into the sky, illuminating the dark clouds rolling over Erin's Glen. Duly fortified by her morning beverage, she zipped up her coat, pushed her feet into her boots, and clipped the lead onto Ziggy's collar. She was off up the hill.

She saw the blue lights in the distance and carried on in their direction. In a way, she was unsurprised to see some police presence in this area of natural beauty that was a source of rumour and contention. With all the recent fuss about the proposed development up there, there was bound to be some trouble. She hoped it was nothing serious. Maybe it was just another protest.

As she got closer, she felt an ominous sense of foreboding. There were a lot of strong feelings in the town about the proposed development. Many of those struggling with an economic downturn in business felt the tourist centre would breathe new life into the town and help pick up its flagging prosperity. Others said that the planned building project was nothing short of blasphemy. Passions ran deep, and Rosie suddenly felt nervous about what might have happened there. She chided herself for not switching on the radio news that morning.

As she got closer, Ziggy suddenly stopped abruptly. He stood, ears twitching and nose up, sniffing. His little body stiffened. He began to make a low growling noise. Rosie stopped patiently and surveyed her dog. She knew him well enough to respect these signs of his alarm. Indeed, the skin prickled on the back of her neck, and she shivered despite her heavy waxed coat, thick jumper, joggers, and boots.

'Well, we're here now; we might as well go and see what's going on.'

Ziggy glanced up at his owner as if seeking reassurance and trotted on. He looked anxiously from left to right and glanced back at her.

As Rosie drew nearer, she could see a familiar stocky figure – Dan, the police officer, at the entrance gate by the forest.

As she approached, he greeted Rosie with an upraised hand and a nod, 'Alright there, Rosie, I'm afraid there is no access through the forest today.' Seeing that she was looking blankly at him, he continued, 'There was a body found early this morning.'

'Dear Lord, who was it?' Rosie put her gloved hand to her heart, shocked to hear the news. Her lined face registered her genuine concern.

'I'm sorry, Rosie, but that news hasn't yet been released to the public.' In truth, Dan felt uncomfortable treating Rosie as just another member of the public. She had been instrumental in helping the local police in the past, and he did not want to leave her out of this investigation either. Her intuition, sharp recall of detail and memory were all talents that were helpful to him and the team at the local station. Dan stepped closer to her and looked behind him to ensure no one was eavesdropping on their conversation. He inclined his head towards Rosie as his eyes slid either side, 'What I can tell you is that your friend Mary Jo discovered the body.'

Dan looked Rosie in the eye, and she got his point; he couldn't tell her who it was, but perhaps Mary Jo could.

'Right, so, thanks, Dan.' Rosie nodded. Despite the understanding she had with Dan, she respected professional boundaries and was reluctant to get him into any bother with his superiors. So, with these considerations in mind, she cut the conversation short and confirmed that she would be getting on her way.

Rosie turned back toward her bungalow. Just then, one of the police cars up at the fort passed her on the road. She saw Mary Jo in the back seat. The nun raised her hand to greet her pal, and Rosie quickly put her clenched hand to her own ear, indicating she would ring her soon.

Rosie felt sorry that her kind and gentle friend had experienced such a shock. Even Mary Jo would need to take a day off work after that happened.

As Rosie rounded onto the street where she lived, she explored the various possibilities concerning the deceased's identity. Maybe it was someone from the protest group? They had been causing enough disruption in the town recently, but it was not enough for someone to want to do away with them. I hope to God it wasn't that poor soul Toddy, she mused. She felt sorry for the isolated man up there living in that half-derelict cottage. For a brief second, it flashed into her mind that it could be Father Asher. He was building up a reputation for himself that not everyone approved of. In truth, she was a bit dubious herself about his viewpoints and style of expressing his faith. She couldn't imagine the builder Sam Bazley letting anyone get the better of him. He was a towering hulk of a man that few would want to take on. She knew Fiona Fitzgerald, the Erin's Glen representative in Brussels, was over there now, so she was out of the picture. With a sudden dawning realisation, she deduced who it was. She could guess why. But who? Who would feel so strongly about the proposed development that they would be motivated to kill someone?

As Rosie stepped inside her bungalow, she turned and bolted the door behind her. She looked out the large window of her lounge for a moment, which gave a sweeping view of the glen. Spectacular on a clear day. It was grey and muted this morning. Despite it being past sunrise, the sky was heavy and dark. Vast blobs of rain spattered against the glass, and the whistle and sigh of the wind catching the corner of her bungalow created an eerie accompaniment to the troubling questions that filled Rosie's mind.

CHAPTER TEN

Shocking News

Later that morning, at the bookshop and café, Deirdre stood at the threshold of the kitchen and shop with her hands on her hips. 'Would you look at that?' She shook her head and smiled in a mock-exasperated fashion at Willow-Patch's antics. Marie abandoned her task of restocking a shelf of exercise books to stroll closer for a look.

'I told him to stay out of the kitchen while I was preparing food. And look at him. He's a case, all right!'

Willow-Patch, in true feline style, was making a point. He was sitting on the boundary line between the kitchen and shop. His body was in the shop, but he had extended his tail into the kitchen. He sat glaring at Deirdre with his tail tapping angrily just inside the forbidden territory. Both women were now laughing at him as the bell on the shop door tinkled, heralding the arrival of the first customer of the morning.

'Good morning, Mrs Blaney. Are you quiet up at the B&B then?' Deirdre called over to the B&B proprietor, who liked to pop into the café when she was not in demand at her guest house.

'Yes indeed, Deirdre, I don't often get much time to myself, as you know, but I do like to support local business, so I thought I'd pay you a visit and see how things are with you two girls.' Mrs Blaney stood, slowly removing her gloves as she looked around the shop. 'Very quiet in here this morning. I hope everything is––'

Mrs Blaney's observations were interrupted by the next customer bustling in, eager to escape the heavy rain shower that had just started.

Trish O'Hara stood in the doorway momentarily, back to the shop, shaking out her umbrella and then turning inwards. As usual, Trish was beaming with a broad smile, but it froze as she entered, clearly not too enamoured at an impromptu meeting with the B&B owner.

Trish quickly rearranged her fallen face and said, 'What a morning! I've got soaked to the skin. I've just dropped Roisin off at school, and I thought I'd treat myself to a nice hot cup of tea and a wee treat before I went to the hair salon myself. Alright there, Mrs B?' Trish nodded and sat down at the table closest to the kitchen, keen to chat with the establishment's owners.

'How is Roisin?' Marie enquired, referring to Trish's seven-year-old daughter.

'Ah, she's not too bad, thanks for asking. But she's got wind of the news. She's uptight about building on the fairy ring. I blame her daddy; I should say her daddy's mammy, her Granny Agnes. She's been filling her head with all sorts of stories about the little people and the revenge they will take on the people of Erin's Glen if the Ring is disturbed. She's been having nightmares about it. She believes that the fairies live inside the mound and that if pushed out, they'll come into the town, steal away the babies, and play tricks on all the people. And--'

The usually chatty and cheerful Trish cut her words short, overcome with concern for her little girl.

Mrs Blaney was following the conversation with apparent interest. Her eyes were large behind her glasses, and her arched eyebrows indicated a perpetual expression of anticipation.

'I know no good will come of it. You just wait and see' Mrs Blaney claimed her seniority in the small group by sitting up tall on her seat and wagging her figure at the younger women.

They looked at her briefly, and after a second of respectful silence, the conversation turned back to the neutral topic of the inclement weather.

Deirdre returned to her duties in the kitchen, and Marie took the orders for tea and toasted tea cakes. The local radio station was playing U2 in the background, and Marie and Deirdre hummed along as they brewed the tea and set out the tea things on two pretty trays. Mrs Blaney occupied herself by rummaging through her enormous handbag. Trish sat quietly, tapping her foot to the music and looking around the shop in silence.

The music on the radio in the kitchen stopped, and the familiar jingle announced the local news bulletin. The smooth tones of the news presenter drifted into the bookshop.

'Good morning. We've had dramatic news this morning from Erin Glen. Dervla Molloy is at the scene now. What can you tell us, Dervla?'

'Good morning, Barry. Yes, I'm at the fairy ring in Erin's Glen now. The scenes here are chaotic. I can see multiple police cars and an ambulance, and I can tell you that the immediate area around the fort has been cordoned off. Apparently, in the early hours of this morning, a body was discovered upon the fort. Ah, here is Seargent Kennedy now--'

There was a break in the reception from the news reporter on the scene, and the radio station announcer apologised for the break in contact.

'That's all we have from Dervla for now. We will return to that story before the end of the bulletin.'

Mrs Blaney's features were set in a grim expression. She shook her head slowly, absorbing the shocking news with an 'I told you so' look on her face.

The younger women looked around at each other in alarm.

Trish was the first to speak. 'A body? Who could it be? Dear God, surely no one would feel strongly enough about a mound of earth to murder someone?'

'It could just be natural causes,' Deirdre offered. 'Maybe someone up there out for a run or a walk and took ill, a heart attack or something...' Deirdre trailed off, realising that this was wishful thinking and that it was unlikely such a heavy police presence would have been needed if it was a collapsed jogger or dog walker.

Trish started to speak, 'I--'

'Shush!' Mrs Blaney put her finger to her lips as Trish gave her a dark look. The four women looked to the radio as the news bulletin returned to the scene at the hill fort.

'We've re-established the connection with Dervla at the scene in Erin's Glen. What can you tell us, Dervla?'

'Thanks, Barry, I've got Sergeant Kennedy here with me now, and he has kindly agreed to give us a statement, Sergent Kennedy...'

Sergeant Kennedy took a second to clear his throat, 'Aye, mm well, we can't say much at the moment.'

'I believe a body was discovered upon the fort this morning, is that right?' the reporter prompted.

'Yes, that's correct. A jogger discovered the body at 6.45 am today.' The police officer confirmed; there was a few seconds of silence, and then Dervla cut back in, 'Tell us, was it foul play?'

'Well, due to the way the body was found, we can conclude that the death was not spontaneous. The extremely wet weather this morning has hampered our investigations.'

'How do you mean you believe the death was not spontaneous? Are we talking murder here, Sergeant Kennedy?' The reporter pressed for more information.

'I'm afraid I cannot say anything more about the situation. Giving out further details may jeopardise the case. I'm sorry. Good day to you.'

'So, there you have it, Barry. That's all the information we have to date. I'll stay at the scene and hopefully bring you more of an update in the next bulletin.'

'We will, of course, give you updates as we get them.' The radio station announcer continued with a weather forecast and a round-up of the forthcoming sports fixtures for the weekend. Marie snapped the radio off.

The small group in the café remained silent; Mrs Blaney blinked behind her glasses, and Trish sat pale-faced, gazing out at the rain battering the shop window. Deirdre and Marie exchanged concerned glances. A heavy, cold silence descended on the shop, broken only by the wind that whistled down the street, smashing sheets of rain up against the window and tugging at the shop door.

Willow-Patch strolled into the shop and meowed piteously, obviously unsettled by the unusual silence.

Chapter Eleven

Craft, Cake and Conversation

A regular bright spot in the week for some of the Erin's Glen inhabitants was the weekly craft group held at Marie and Deirdre's café. The two women had hosted the craft evening for a few months, and it had been a source of support, pleasure, and sociability for the group of friends who attended most Wednesdays. Despite the chilling news of the day, they decided to open their doors to the group as usual that evening. They decided they could do with a bit of light relief from the heaviness of the day's news.

The craft group produced many beautiful items, usually with a seasonal theme. Various celebrations punctuated the year in Erin's Glen, a mishmash of old Celtic celebrations, religious observances, and traditional cultural events. The group had been preparing for the next big date on the Erin's Glen calendar, which was May Day. Every year, a bonfire would take place on the last night of April, followed by a big parade and celebrations the following day. The winters were long in Erin's Glen, and the locals welcomed spring with exuberance.

Rosie was a regular attendee and contributor to the craft group. Her contributions were mostly snippets of local information and occasional gossip, but she managed to finish some projects in time for the next big occasion. This evening was no exception. It had been unsettling to hear talk of the fairy ring being disturbed for the building of the new tourist centre, and of course, more disturbing still was news of a body found up there. The celebrations might even be postponed this year due to recent events. After some hesitation, she decided to go. Keeping up her routine might help her feel some sense of normality, even if the craft items might not be sold this year. For now, Rosie decided to keep her thoughts about the body's identity to herself. She hadn't heard from Mary Jo, and Rosie hoped she might see her this evening.

It had been a busy week. Father Asher had made an impact on Sunday with a rousing homily about the pitfalls of greed. Quite a few visitors had come to the presbytery to discuss his views directly with the priest. Rosie felt uneasy about the passions the young priest had stirred up as he railed against putting economic progress ahead of the natural environment and the welfare of all creation. Had he inadvertently incited someone to commit a desperate act to halt the building project? These thoughts occupied Rosie's mind as she got ready to go out.

Ziggy recognised her large craft bag and knew he would be home alone that evening. He whimpered with disappointment and retreated to his basket with mournful resignation. He curled up and tucked his nose into his front paws.

'Are you sulking at me?' Rosie called to him as she gathered up her belongings.

Ziggy kept his nose tucked into his paws. She heard a sigh in reply to her question. Rosie switched on the radio for her canine companion and called out, 'See you later' as she closed the front door.

A few minutes later, Rosie had made the short car journey down to Marie and Deirdre's café. As usual, she pulled up outside in her Mini with her customary screech of the brakes and a jolt. She paused to look up at the clear night sky. The last few traces of orange streaks from the setting sun were visible, and a crescent moon was rising. The crisp, cold night air blew her wispy hair gently as she approached the front door. The warmth hit her as she entered, welcomed by the familiar tinkle of the shop bell.

Marie called out from the kitchen, 'Alright there, Rosie? I've got the tea all brewed up for you.'

Deirdre had been sitting at a table in the café and stood up to greet her friend, 'It's been terrible news today, Rosie. Are you alright?' Deirdre asked as she stroked Rosie's arm, looking into the older woman's eyes.

Rosie nodded, although she felt a lump in her throat. She quickly produced her latest culinary creations to move the conversation on to more mundane matters. Rosie proffered her box of cakes.

'I know they look a bit odd,' Rosie explained as Deirdre, now joined by Marie, peered into the large Tupperware box full of oddly shaped treats.

'I got a new cupcake maker. You know how I am with technology...' Rosie looked at her friends. They nodded slowly, realising that a Rosie-technical-hitch story was about to unfold. 'Well, I got the settings wrong. It was not my fault. I don't know why the buttons have white markings on a white background. But anyway, to cut a long story short, they came out upside down with the frosting on the bottom.'

'Ah, never worry. Sure, they all go down the same way.' Deirdre declared. She went back to the kitchen to fetch the tea. Rosie and Marie settled down by a table. Marie picked up some knitting as they waited.

Rosie pushed her glasses up her nose as she looked at what Marie had picked up to work on.

'Ah, sure, would you look at these?' she exclaimed as she moved closer to pick up some tiny, knitted rosebuds that Marie had already produced. 'These are beautiful.'

Marie smiled back at Rosie in appreciation for the compliment.

'Well, I believe we have a floral theme for the parade in May, so I want to do a range of blankets adorned with rosebuds.' Marie tucked away the flowers and wool to make room for the tea tray coming their way. Deirdre placed the large teapot, cups, saucers, plates and a large plate of Rosie's lemon cupcakes in the middle of the table. The usual routine was to have tea and cake and discuss plans for the various projects the women were engaged with. Some of these projects were completed as a group, and some individually. However, the conversation tonight was dominated by the recent local news.

Uncharacteristically, Marie, an incomer from London, prompted the discussion by saying, 'I'm so upset about what has happened. Everything feels so...' she searched for the right word, '... troubled. All this talk of disturbing the fairy ring and now, this horrible thing––' Marie finished abruptly, clearly very emotional about recent events.

'I think many of us are love.' Rosie shook her head grimly. 'My mother always said that messing with the little people was bad luck. I'm not a superstitious woman, but I can't help but think any disturbance up there is bad news.' Rosie was usually cheerful and lively, and her uncharacteristic doom-filled tidings this evening cast a gloom over the gathering.

Deirdre had returned with the tea and joined in the discussion, 'You're right, Rosie, sure look at all the trouble with that factory over in Belfast.'

The other two women nodded slowly, recalling events from a few years back.

Deirdre continued, 'Aye, you remember, DeLorean, that Yankee businessman who opened that car factory. He was told it was in a fairy ring, and he ignored the warnings, built the factory and sure look how all that turned out...'

The venture had been a disaster, and Deirdre didn't need to say anymore.

Marie brought the conversation back to local events, 'Well, Gerry Macauley seems all for it. Fiona Fitzgerald is backing it, too. She's getting the funding. They both say it will bring tourists into the town.'

'Sure, we're doing just fine without the tourists.' Rosie was always thankful that Erin's Glen was not on the tourist trail and enjoyed the peace the small town offered.

'And now this.' Marie looked off into the distance.

The ladies sat quietly for a moment, absorbing the day's events.

Deirdre sighed, 'No Mary Jo this evening. Sister Angela popped in earlier to say she wasn't feeling up to it.'

Rosie felt a stab of disappointment, but she wasn't surprised. Her friend had had a terrible shock. She had telephoned Riverside House earlier but was told Mary Jo was resting. A few of the other locals were missing this evening, too.

Just then, the conversation was halted by the appearance of Willow-Patch, the pet cat belonging to Marie and Deirdre. He had decided to make a dramatic entrance by jumping gracefully up onto the back of Marie's chair and prancing delicately from one chair back to the next in a feline acrobatic display.

'Well, look at you, the entertainer,' Marie scooped him up affectionately, and he settled on her lap, looking around the assembled group with an expectant look.

'Oh, go on, then.' Deirdre poured some milk from the little jug into a saucer. Willow-Patch looked at it with disdain and, after a few moments, languidly slipped off Marie's lap and padded over to the milk.

The rest of the evening passed pleasantly enough, with the radio playing softly in the background. The crafters were quiet tonight, subdued by the recent news and their reduced group size.

While Marie was washing up in the kitchen, Rosie asked Deirdre, 'Do you know much about that boyo who runs the antique shop?'

Deirdre looked at her friend, 'You mean Cornelius Quinn?' She replied.

'Aye, that's him. I can never remember his name. Anyway, I was just wondering if you knew much about him. He went off a few years back and then returned to Erin's Glen to set up the shop, but where did he go? I never knew what he was doing. He's a bit of an enigma.'

Suddenly, there was a loud clatter of smashing crockery from the kitchen.

'Are you alright there? Deirdre called over to Marie. As Rosie and Deirdre rushed to the crash scene, Willow-Patch whipped past their ankles with a giant blob of yellow-coloured icing on his head.

'Oh, it's nothing, just Willow-Patch being greedy.' Marie was bent down, picking up pieces of a broken plate, its fragments interspersed amongst the debris of smashed lemon cakes and icing on the floor. Deirdre stooped to help clear up. Rosie realised she would have to find out more about Cornelius another time.

With a heavy sense of foreboding and dread, Rosie gathered up her belongings. Despite the evening's company, chat, tea, and pleasant occupations, Rosie couldn't shake off her anxiety about developments in Erin's Glen.

As Rosie drove home, the sense of foreboding increased. Her thoughts were filled with the various implications of the latest developments in town. Gerry Macauley had gone very quiet over the past few days. What had he been up to? Fiona Fitzgerald, the local Member of the European Parliament, was in Brussels in the final stages of securing funding for the tourist centre. If she secured the funding, would that mean the diggers would be moving into the fairy fort sometime soon? If so, was Sam Bazley of S.B. Builders going to build it? Was Gerry only interested in bringing business to the town, or did he have a personal stake in the building project? Who would gain most from it being built? How far would the protestors go to stop its construction? Would the protestors go so far as to do away with someone to stop the construction?

Suddenly, Rosie had to slam her foot down on the brake and screeched to a halt in the centre of the deserted road. She had become so absorbed in her thoughts that her attention had drifted. The appearance of an ephemeral figure in front of her in the middle of the road had shocked her back into full focus. The figure had now disappeared back into the trees. The car had stalled. Rosie felt her heart thud violently in her chest as she sat in the immobile vehicle. The dark seemed to close in around her. An owl hooting punctuated the silence. Rosie had to take a few deep breaths before her trembling hands could turn the ignition key and put the car back into gear. Shaken by the strange apparition, Rosie continued her journey, eager to get back to the cheerful familiarity of her neat little bungalow.

Chapter Twelve

Nightmares in the Woods

A few nights before the shocking discovery in the fairy ring, Toddy was already troubled. He lay in his hard, single bed with the covers up to his eyes. His hands grasped desperately onto the threadbare edge of the blanket. His knuckles showed up a luminous white in the moonlight that filtered through the ragged net curtains on the small, grimy window. Toddy's eyes were shut tight, and he lay so tensely that sleep was impossible. He got up and stumbled about the room, feeling around for the box of matches with one hand as he found a stub of a candle with the other. He struck the match, and the small light exploded momentarily in the icy darkness, making his steamy breath visible in the frigid air. He put the lit match to the candle with a shaking hand. He felt chilled to the bone despite his thick, long johns and the scratchy, old, woollen dressing gown he wore to bed.

Toddy got up from the bed and shuffled along with the flickering candle held aloft, pushing his feet through a residue of socks, odd shoes, and discarded clothing. Toddy lived alone and rarely felt the urge to tidy up. The air was stale and fusty. The piles of books, newspapers and jumbles of disparate items created dark shadows that played on the walls.

The cottage was a single-story affair, and he didn't have far to go to reach the kitchen area. He placed the flickering candle amongst some scattered cups and plates and filled the old kettle, battered, and blackened from decades of use on the open fire. He had connected a gas bottle to his old cooker that day. The blue flame of the gas warmed him as it licked around the kettle's base. He lifted the teapot and peered in; the tealeaf dregs were still damp, and he could reuse them. He looked at an unfamiliar paper bag of loose tea and threw it in the fireplace. Toddy's blue eyes were red-rimmed, and he rubbed his hand down over his bearded face, scratching at the raspy, thick stubble. His dark, curly hair stood up at odd angles.

As the kettle began to bubble and whistle, he sighed deeply. Would he ever get a decent night's sleep again? Since that night out on the road, the *Shee* had haunted his dreams and tormented him.

He had let them down. He had failed to keep them and their secrets safe. Self-loathing and reproach gnawed at his insides and tormented his dreams. Sleep was elusive, and his days had passed in an endless, edgy compulsion to keep watch at the fairy ring.

He had one friend in the town – not his drinking pals, who were only good for a bit of banter and light-hearted craic that meant nothing. He had only one *real* friend who understood his mission and role. He needed to protect the town and himself, and his friend would help him. Maybe then, when all this business was settled, he would get some sleep.

The sound of the whistling kettle broke into his reverie. The gush and gurgle of the boiling water as he filled up the old teapot comforted him. He could remember many family meals when that teapot was on the table. On special occasions like birthdays and festival days, his mother would make a big dinner, and they would all sit around the table, his parents laughing and telling stories. His father would sometimes break out the whiskey and scratch a few tunes on the fiddle. The child Toddy would sit on his mother's knee as she jiggled him up and down in time to the music, clapping his tiny, chubby hands inside hers in rhythm with the jaunty tunes.

Those memories sharply contrasted with Toddy's cold, lonely existence in the old cottage. The images and sounds from the past were echoes that seemed to come and go. Even these happy memories now tortured Toddy. His parents had put their faith and trust in him. He was the keeper of the fairy ring, just like his father had been. But unlike his father, he was making a mess of it. Self-reproach curdled in his stomach and created a sour taste in his mouth.

'Some keeper you are!' Toddy mocked himself. He took a slug of tea that washed away some of the bile and warmed his stomach.

The candle wavered, vulnerable in the ancient draughty cottage. He stared at the flame that danced in the soft breeze, mesmerised by its blue-yellow light.

Toddy cradled his tea a while longer, dreading another attempt to sleep in the cold, narrow bed in the room at the back of the house. He decided to sit down in the chair by the fireplace. The old chair was stuffed with horsehair that poked through the worn fabric. The hearth, which often served as his cooker, was cold tonight. A few grey, burnt-out coals sat above a pile of powdery ashes. Despite the chilly air and uncomfortable seat, Toddy put his head back and was soon in a deep slumber brought on by days out in the open, keeping watch over the fairy ring and many sleepless nights. He dreamt of weird creatures, half-animal and human. He saw them pouring out from an opening in the mound of the fairy ring and spilling out into the town, creating havoc, stealing babies and charming men. Toddy cried out in his sleep, his arms flaying about and his legs jerking erratically. In his dream, he is fighting with a savage beast; its claw-like hands are around his neck, and he is gasping for air – Toddy lurched back suddenly into consciousness.

As he sat bolt upright in the chair, breathing heavily, he sensed that he was not alone. A few silent moments passed. He heard tapping at a windowpane in the cottage. He looked over at the kitchen window above the sink. He could see a few streaks of early morning light stippling across the mackerel-like cloud. He sat and waited. The tapping started again – tap, tap, tap – then stopped. Toddy strained his ears to try to determine which direction it was coming from. Tap, tap, tap. It sounded like it came from the back of the house. Toddy gripped the arms of the chair and took a breath as he stood up suddenly, determined to find out where the unnerving noise was coming from. He ran into the back bedroom. It was as he left it. The pale light of dawn illuminated it – a grey-monochrome version of his untidy room.

The silence closed in again.

Tap, tap, tap – now it sounds like it's at the front. He runs back into the kitchen, grabbing the poker from the fireplace as he dashes to the window.

Nothing.

He stands momentarily, scratching his head in confusion, feeling powerless and persecuted. He drops the poker and puts both his hands to his head – tap, tap, tap – is it inside his head or at a window? His bewildered torment intensifies as he shakes his head and begins to moan – 'Leave me alone.'

Chapter Thirteen

Stirring Memories

The blue light from the television screen flashed across the faces of Marie and Deirdre as they sat together in their cosy lounge above the café and bookstore. It was early evening, and they had shut up shop for the day. Willow-Patch was sprawled out on the sofa between them, taking up more than his fair share of the sofa, with both women squashed up against each armrest on either side. Marie was busy knitting, and Deirdre was flicking through a cookery book, seeking inspiration for some sweet new treats to bake for the café.

It had been a busy day. Dramatic news in the town always seemed to stir the local population to gather in meeting places for a natter about what was going on. Marie and Deirdre had grown weary of the repetitive questions and wild rumours and had decided to close a little earlier than usual, come upstairs, and wait for the news. Both had become absorbed in their preoccupations as they sat in front of the television with the volume on low.

The only sounds in the room were Marie's clicking knitting needles, crackles from the wood burner and the barely perceptible murmuring from the television.

Marie finished a row of knitting and put her needles down to one side.

'I don't really understand the fuss about building on the fort,' she pronounced.

Deirdre looked up from her book and responded, 'How do you mean?'

'Well, I appreciate the concerns about disturbing a historical site, but all this talk of the *Shee* – of fairies and what-not – surely it's all just silly superstition!'

'Yes, but you don't appreciate how powerful that superstition is. It's less than one hundred years since a woman was burned alive because she was suspected of being a fairy – or a witch. The two seem to have been melded into one supernatural being – the *Shee*. Irish fairies are not like your English garden variety! They have a meaner reputation, and people are frightened.'

'Who got burned as a witch or a fairy then?' Marie queried, intrigued.

'Brigid Cleary, down in Cloneen, near Clonmel in Tipperary. It only happened in 1895. We used to sing a skipping rhyme at school. Do you know those rhymes set to a skipping rhythm?' Deirdre clapped her hands as if in time to steady skips over a skipping rope.

Marie nodded. It brought back memories of jumping over a rope with school friends at playtime.

Deirdre clapped in time again as she chanted the rhyme, 'It went: " Witch or fairy, are you the wife of Michael Cleary?" Michael Cleary put his wife, Brigid, on fire to prove if she was really Brigid the woman or a changeling – a fairy witch. The poor woman died of her burns.

It's a horrible story, but it makes you realise how strong feelings are about all of this.'

Marie shuddered, disturbed by Deirdre's recollection of this true story.

The evening news brought their attention back to the screen. Deirdre hopped off the sofa to switch up the volume. Both sat with faces alert as more details about the news of the body found in the fairy ring were shared with the nation. Even Willow-Patch sat bolt upright now, alarmed by the sudden tension in the air as his humans concentrated on the television.

They had been following the news on the radio for most of the day, keen to find out the identity of the body. A tight police presence had been kept at the scene, and an even tighter hold on information was in place. Even Mrs Blaney had to admit she was still not privy to the identity of the body. Speculation had been rife. There was also considerable discussion about how the corpse had been found; Seargent Kennedy had let slip that there was something unusual in how it had been arranged. All sorts of theories were voiced as to what that might mean.

'Well, I reckon most of Erin's Glen will be glued to the news tonight.' Deirdre fell silent as the news reporter began to allude to the revelation of the deceased person's identity.

'We've just had confirmation that the body has been identified and the family informed. Over to Dervla now, who is in Erin's Glen. Dervla, what can you tell us?'

A very cold-looking reporter was standing outside Erin's Glen police station, muffled up in a heavy scarf and hat, spoke into a fuzzy-headed microphone, 'Yes, Barry, Sergeant Kennedy has confirmed that he can now make a statement, and he is here with us now, Seargent––'

Dervla swung the microphone around to a stony-faced Sergeant Kennedy, who was looking fixedly at the camera. He had a piece of paper in his hand and looked down at it with concentration as he read slowly: 'I can confirm that this morning, the body of Gerry Macauley, the Erin's Glen councillor, was found on the hill fort, known locally as the fairy ring in a wooded area close to the town. I can also confirm that due to the nature of his demise, we are pursuing a murder investigation. We are appealing to anyone with any information relevant to Mr Macauley's death to come forward and speak with the police. We can be contacted at Erin's Glen police station.'

'Thank you, Seargent Kennedy.' Dervla swung away from the police officer and back to face the camera. 'Well, there you have it, disturbing news from Erin's Glen today. A town in shock.'

The camera then panned out to show Erin's Glen high street, quiet in the twilight, with just a few lights on in accommodation above shops – just like the flat where Deirdre and Marie sat now.

They looked at each other wide-eyed. The full impact of the news sinking in. Deirdre gasped.

'What is it?' Marie asked urgently.

'Well, it might be nothing...'

Marie waited patiently.

'But...' Deirdre frowned. 'Ah, maybe it was nothing.'

'What?' Marie asked again, with a bit more of an edge to her tone.

Dierdre sighed, 'Well, last week...it was about this time of the evening I saw Gerry Macauley coming down the street. He'd just got out of his fancy car. I thought he was heading down to the fish and chip shop for his tea. I often saw him doing that, especially on a Friday night.'

'Okay, you saw him go for fish and chips?' Marie was frowning, trying to see the relevance.

'Yes, but he didn't go into the fish bar. He stepped into the doorway of the shop here. It was like he wanted to have a quiet word with someone and didn't want to be seen on the street.'

Marie continued to listen patiently, nodding in encouragement as Deirdre continued.

'He was talking to someone quietly, to begin with, and then his voice got louder as if he was angry with the person he was speaking with. He was talking with a man; initially, I saw him only in outline as it was getting dark. The conversation was getting quite heated. I remember I pulled back a bit into the shop I didn't want them to see me in case they got angry with me.'

'Who was Gerry Macauley talking to?' Marie asked, her eyes fixed on Deirdre's face as she recalled what she had seen the previous week.

'I'm just trying to think of his name. You know that big fellow that works with Seamus from up the road…ah, what's his name…' Deirdre shook her head, trying to dislodge the memory.

'Ah, I know, that chap with the tan…' Marie started.

'Aye, that's the man himself.' Deirdre nodded.

Just then, there was an insistent ring on the doorbell from downstairs.

'That'll be the guard's doing their door-to-door calls. I'll go down and tell them what I know; if I don't remember his name, they will.' Deirdre jumped up off the sofa. Willow-Patch, still sitting bolt-upright, followed her with his alert green eyes. He glanced back at Marie and settled back down, curling his front paws under his chest, ears pricked, listening to the conversation that floated up the stairs from the shop's front door below them. His ears twitched like antennae, adjusting to the different voices.

Marie got up and switched off the television set. She, too, was listening carefully. She could hear the low rumble of the police officers' deep voices interspersed with Deirdre's lighter tones. A few words from the police officer broke a short silence, and then she heard Deirdre shout, 'Yes, that's it!' More conversation rumbled on at a lower volume, and then the door banged shut.

Deirdre clattered back up the wooden stairs, looking flushed.

'They've asked me to pop down to the station tomorrow. As it happens, they think what I saw is very significant.' Deirdre shrugged, and both women looked at each other seriously. Marie shivered and stood up abruptly, walking towards the window that overlooked the street below.

'What on earth has been going on right under our noses.' Marie shook her head as she glanced out the window and pulled the curtains shut.

Chapter Fourteen

Protests

The following Sunday, most of the residents of Erin's Glen attended Mass at St Bridget's church, a neo-Gothic building complete with colourful stained glass windows. Although Rosie was not a fan of the new young priest, she *was* a dutiful parishioner. So, she ensured Ziggy had a good walk before she set off to attend church as usual.

Rosie threw her large handbag onto the passenger seat of her Mini; as she did so, she caught sight of Ziggy looking forlornly out the front window of her bungalow. Rosie waved at him and felt a stab of guilt leaving him behind.

'He'll be alright for an hour. You spoil that dog rotten!' Kay, Rosie's neighbour and friend, was also on her way to Mass. Rosie turned quickly to face her.

'Ach, sure, don't I know all about it! Would you like a lift, Kay? I take it you are heading down to Mass yourself?' Rosie lifted her bag to accommodate Kay, who willingly accepted the offer.

Kay was a teacher at the local girls' school. Recent news had upset the pupils, and Kay had a difficult week trying to keep them focused on their studies.

'Terrible news this week.' Kay began shaking her head. 'I wonder what will happen with the building of this new project, the ––'

Rosie didn't get a chance to answer as she had to brake suddenly to avoid hitting a crowd that had gathered on the road. The group were a rag-tag-looking bunch. Rosie thought most of them looked like they could do with a good wash. Rosie hovered her foot over the accelerator, ready to zoom off quickly. As she wound down the window, a young man with long dreadlocks and a camouflage-style jacket approached the side of the car. He had leaflets in his hand, as did his companions, and they were stopping other vehicles, handing out the pamphlets and engaging drivers and passersby in conversation.

'Good morning, sorry to bother you, Mrs––'

The young man smiled. Rosie was a bit distracted by his nose ring but managed to inform him of her name.

'*Miss* O'Riley,' Rosie answered. She thought he was a bit too young to be calling her Rosie.

'Miss O'Riley, I'm sure you have heard about the proposed building up on the fort?'

Rosie nodded, surprised this lot had the cheek to be out after the news from the fairy ring that week. She was also keen to move on; she didn't want to be late for Mass. She stuck her hand out to take the leaflet and put her foot down on the accelerator as the young man jumped back, clearly not accustomed to Rosie's style of decisive driving.

Rosie handed the leaflet to her passenger. Kay opened the threefold A4 sheet.

'Oh, I've seen this already. Loads of them are around the town. I can't believe they're still handing them out after what happened.'

The leaflet was photocopied from a handwritten sheet, complete with some shaky sketches of the hill fort and trees. Kay read out a few paragraphs.

Preserve Our Heritage: Save Our Ancient Hill Fort!

Say NO to the Tourist Centre on Our Sacred Land!

Dear Fellow Guardians of Heritage,

We stand united in the fight to protect our beloved ancient hill fort from the threat of a tourist centre. This cherished site, a testament to Ireland's rich history and cultural heritage, should be safeguarded, not commercialised.

'Well, they seem harmless enough. You can't blame them for trying to save the fort.' Kay commented.

'That's all very well, but what can we do?' Rosie queried.

Kay scanned the leaflet and looked for some action points. 'Blah, blah...mmm...well, it says here we can "attend public meetings, sign the petition and raise awareness with friends and family." But sure, will it make any difference?' Kay queried. 'It probably won't happen now with Gerry gone anyway. However, I suppose Fiona is still in the case. She seems mad keen to get this thing built.'

Rosie bit her lip regretfully, looking in her rearview mirror, 'Oh, right. That lad was trying to get me to sign something back there. Ah, well, I'll go back later. Right-o, here we are.' Rosie glanced at the leaflet, noted the handwritten script, and popped it into her bag.

Kay looked back at the ragtag-looking bunch of protestors and said to Rosie, 'Do you think *they've* had anything to do with Gerry's death?'

Rosie didn't answer as the car jerked forward. Rosie pulled hard on the handbrake outside the church. Both women got out, smiling and waving at the other parishioners rushing into Mass.

'Well, let's see what his nibs has to say for himself this morning.' Rosie was referring to Asher Callaghan, the new parish priest.

'You're not a fan then?' Kay smiled.

'I respect the cloth but not the man.' Rosie replied loftily.

Both women noted that several younger people filled the pews inside the church this morning, which was unusual. Usually, those under the age of twenty-five lurked about at the back, standing by the doors, ready to scurry off as soon as Communion was over. But this morning, there were many expectant, fresh faces in the pews at the front.

A folk group piped up from the back, complete with guitars, a flute and a small handheld drum. A cheerful, rousing tune announced the priest's entrance.

The readings from the bible that morning were from Genesis and The Book of Ecclesiastes. Father Asher warmed up his parishioners with the message of good stewardship of the earth. He then moved on to rail against how the planet was being ravaged by greedy exploitation. Many congregation members that morning were stirred by Father Asher's passionate tirade against the ruthless pursuit of profit. Usually a mild-mannered man, he seemed to thunder out his sermon today.

'Whoever loves money never has enough; whoever loves wealth is never satisfied with their income. This, too, is meaningless.'

He left a few moments of reflective silence, which added to the drama of the words from scripture. It struck Rosie as very odd that Father Asher did not refer to the body found the previous day. She looked around her. Many of the younger people were smiling and nodding. Some other locals sat stony-faced. A few parishioners seemed to slink down in their seats. As she peered around to the back, she saw that Sam Beazley, the builder, had snuck in the back, standing with a grim expression on his bronzed face, his gold medallion glinting in the sunlight that streamed in through the stained glass windows. It was hard to read Sam's expression. Rosie turned her attention back to Father Asher, then glanced back at Sam Bazley.

He was gone.

Chapter Fifteen

Sharing Knowledge

Grey clouds rolled over Erin's Glen the following day. Rosie had slept poorly. She woke up feeling groggy and heavy-headed, and when she saw the uninspiring weather, she felt like getting back under the covers and going back to sleep. However, two bright golden eyes looked at her indignantly; Ziggy stood at the foot of the bed and gave a little yelp.

'Alright, alright. No rest for the wicked.' Rosie sighed and shuffled into her slippers, following her curly-haired little dog into the kitchen to fill the kettle and give him his breakfast. She was ready for work after going through her familiar morning routine more slowly than usual. Her lethargy that morning meant there was no time for a walk, Ziggy having to make do with a quick scoot around the garden. He stood hopefully by the front door as his owner shrugged into her coat.

On impulse, Rosie decided to take her canine pet to work today despite the risk of a frenzied encounter with her boss's stray cat. 'Okay, then, let's go.' Ziggy trotted after his owner and hopped into the Mini.

When Rosie settled herself behind the wheel, a flashback of the figure from the other evening dominated her vision again. After the latest news, she felt even more unsettled by this encounter. She squared her shoulders and took a deep breath. 'Come on, girl, it takes more than some youngster playing tricks in a white dress to shake you,' she chastised herself.

In truth, Rosie wasn't sure *what* she had seen, but she preferred to think of it as human. She had heard tales of local people being bothered by some inhuman creatures, especially during troubled times, but she had dismissed them as superstitious nonsense until now.

The rattle and throaty rumble of the old Mini's engine soothed her. After the short drive, she arrived outside the priest's house, where the parish office was found. The familiarity of it all helped to settle her sense of unease, and she set about getting on with her workday.

With Ziggy sleeping under the desk in the office, Rosie busied herself with her usual round of typing up letters, completing entries in the parish records, responding to parishioners' enquiries and booking various sacramental services such as baptisms and weddings. Thankfully, there were no funerals that day. There was no sign of Father Asher so far, and she was thinking about making a cup of tea when he strode into the office.

'Good morning, Rosie. Good morning, Ziggy.' Father Asher smiled broadly at his secretary and ducked down to greet Ziggy under the desk. Ziggy, sensing his mistress's ambivalence about the priest, stayed where he was, the only movement being one open eye that glanced up under a wiggly eyebrow.

'Rosie, tell me, is there a CD-ROM drive in that machine there?'

Rosie looked out the window at her car. 'Err, not that I know of.'

Father Asher followed her line of vision and looked at her, confused. He strode over to the computer on her desk. He prodded it with his finger and looked up and down the large tower by the boxy grey-white monitor.

'Ah, that thing...sorry when you talked about a "drive", I thought you meant the car!' Rosie laughed at her own mistake.

Father Asher looked at her uncertainly. With pursed lips and a look of disdain, he concluded, 'Right, well, no worries, I see this ancient thing only has a floppy disk drive.'

Rosie saw the priest holding a shiny, round thing that looked like a coaster. Now, it was her turn to look back at him uncertainly. She was puzzled by his behaviour. He had made no reference to the body found up on the fairy ring. Why was that? The parish secretary watched as Father Asher drifted out of the room with the disc in his hand, mumbling, 'I just needed it to look at some pictures on this thing.'

Rosie wasn't quite sure what *that* was all about. Still, her confusion about the computer reminded her to visit Quinn's Curiosities to pick Cornelius Quinn's brain and get up to speed with spreadsheets – and find out more about the man himself. She looked at the clock. She finished work at 2 pm and would have time to go there before he closed for the day.

'Right Ziggy, best behaviour, you're going to be visiting Mr Quinn this afternoon.'

Ziggy looked unimpressed. He blinked at his owner and settled his nose in his paws again. She heard a deep sigh followed by the low rumble of his doggy snores from under her desk.

An hour later, Rosie was packing up for the day. Ziggy had just appeared from under the desk and was doing a downward dog pose in the middle of the room, stretching after his snooze. He suddenly stood up as if his back had been tweaked upwards with a piece of rope. He tensed and looked from left to right, revealing the whites of his eyes.

His nervous tension had quickly affected his owner, who paused as she got her coat on.

'What is it, wee man?' She looked at him, standing there, quivering. After a second, Rosie laughed and at once relaxed.

'Ah, you furry eegit, it's probably only the cat. I told you, best behaviour; otherwise, you'll get barred!' Rosie chided her canine pal and carried on with her preparations to leave.

She was brought up short by Ziggy's low rumble. It started as a barely audible hum in his throat and then increased in intensity and volume as he stood, growling in the centre of the office.

He looked towards the door and snarled with more ferocity than Rosie had ever heard from him.

'Ziggy!' Even to Rosie's ears, her admonishment sounded weak. Her earlier unease had returned, and she felt a butterfly-like flutter in her stomach. Her mouth went dry, and she realised that her hands were now shaking as she tried to put on her gloves.

'Right, come on now, that's enough.' Rosie marched towards her little dog and grabbed him by the collar; she fished around in her bag for his lead. 'I'm not taking any chances with you, young man.' She attached his lead with a metallic click and stood up to reach for the doorknob.

Rosie opened the door. Ziggy yelped anxiously. For the second time in twenty-four hours, Rosie was shaken to the core by pure fear.

Chapter Sixteen

More Questions than Answers

When Rosie opened the office door, she stepped back and made a sound that surprised even Ziggy. She looked into a pair of slanted green eyes set in a smooth, pale face. Two long blond pigtails fell on either side. Despite Rosie's alarm, the woman stood motionless, her features immobile. A vast grey, shaggy wolfhound stood by her side. It growled ominously.

'Madigan,' the woman uttered the word quickly in a low tone. She kept her gaze fixed on Rosie. The stranger's voice was familiar.

Father Asher stood behind the tall woman, who shimmered white in the hallway's darkness.

'Err, Rosie, this is Sage,' he called behind the statuesque figure.

'Sage and her dog Madigan,' he added. His head popped above the wolfhound. The leggy dog was now glowering at Ziggy, who shrunk back behind Rosie.

Rosie backed into the office to make room for the dogs and humans clustered by the door.

'Pleased to meet you,' Rosie said. Her manners were intuitive, and she put her hand out to Sage, who either ignored it or was unaware as she looked around the office's interior. Rosie was irritated by her superior air and wondered who she was and what she was doing here at St Brigid's. She was a very different character from the average parishioner who visited the priest's house.

As if reading her thoughts, Father Asher explained, 'Sage has been telling me all about the conservation work she has been doing with her group up on the hill fort.' He smiled at Rosie, encouraging her to befriend this unusual woman. Rosie wasn't keen to play along.

'Oh, right so.' Rosie and Sage eyed each other speculatively.

'Rosie is my secretary…keeps me in order!' Father Asher rubbed his hands together and laughed at his self-deprecating comment. Sage didn't even smile.

Usually effusive and friendly, Rosie did not feel inclined to stay in Sage's company. She brought a chilly air into the small, cosy office, and her fair skin, light hair and cream dress exuded a cold luminosity in the poorly lit room. The small square of grey daylight from the north-facing window by the desk provided little light.

'Well, it's lovely to meet you, but I'd best be getting on.' Rosie nearly pushed past the tall woman and pulled Ziggy along. He took the opportunity to glare up defiantly at the wolfhound towering over him. Madigan bared his teeth silently. Rosie gulped and glanced wide-eyed at the hairy hound and his mistress. Once they passed them, Rosie ran across the small hallway out the front door.

It was only a few minutes later that she registered the full impact of the encounter. So, *that* was the figure she had seen in the woods a couple of weeks ago. Although she couldn't be one hundred percent sure, it was most likely also the 'apparition' she had encountered last night. But what was Sage doing out along the road late at night? More to the point, what was she doing at the priest's house?

'What on earth does that priest think he's playing at.' Rosie shook her head in disbelief that this man of the church would be inviting this woman – this *cult leader* into his house. 'Yes, that's it, she must be running some cult up there, and dear God, our parish priest is getting mixed up in it all. What next?' Rosie sighed in exasperation and anxiety about the state of the Church.

As she neared the town, she remembered her earlier resolve to visit Cornelius Quinn for a computer lesson. Always practical, Rosie reckoned that something as down-to-earth as a lesson on spreadsheets would help dispel her misgivings about the strange goings-on in Erin's Glen. With shaking hands, Rosie drove into town and parked outside the antique shop. She took a few breaths to steady herself. She glanced at Ziggy, who wiggled an eyebrow at her as he sat up, looking out onto the street.

'Right now, you've had enough excitement for one day. You can wait in the car.'

Ziggy blinked at her. His honey-coloured eyes looked earnestly at his mistress. He whimpered in agreement and settled down on the seat in resignation.

The Mini was parked outside Quinn's Curiosities, and she marched over with her usual confidence regained. She stopped short as she entered; the bell above the door had tingled announcing her entrance, and a young man with a ponytail and cargo pants strolled out from the back office.

He smiled at her, 'Can I help you?'

For the second time that day, Rosie was taken aback. 'Well, I, um, I was expecting to see Cornelius,' she said.

'Oh, I see!' The young man smiled again. He spoke with a polite English accent.

'I am so sorry Uncle Quinn is out today. I'm Hayden, Hayden Matthews.' Hayden shook hands with Rosie and looked at her expectantly.

'Oh, sorry, yes, I'm Rosie, Rosie O'Reilly. I live in Erin's Glen…' she trailed off uncertainly.

Hayden nodded. Rosie wasn't quite sure how to describe her acquaintance with Cornelius and knew her answer sounded a bit lame.

Hayden didn't seem phased by her hesitancy and said, 'Cornelius is my uncle. I call him "Uncle Quinn;" "Uncle Cornelius" is a bit of a mouthful. I'm visiting from London. Uncle Quinn's sister, Cordelia, is my mother.'

Rosie waited for more information. The pause worked.

The young man continued, '…she moved to London in the 60s and married my dad, Bertie, and, as they say, the rest is history.'

Hayden opened his arms with fingers outstretched, showing that the product of this family history was himself. Then, fixing his gaze on Rosie, he asked, 'Was there anything in particular you needed to discuss with my uncle?'

'Ah, nothing that can't wait.' Rosie suddenly felt very weary from all the unexpected goings-on today. Even her desire to find out more about Hayden was superseded by her need to get home to the quiet familiarity of her bungalow.

'Thanks anyway!' she called out as she turned on her heel and returned to the Mini. Ziggy was already up on his feet, tail wagging, glad to see his mistress back so soon.

As Rosie greeted him and returned to the driver's seat, she paused and looked back into the shop she had just left; why was Hayden here? Was he anything to do with the group up on the hill? How long had he been here, and why was he here now? She could never remember meeting him before and had never heard Cornelius talking about a nephew in London. Rather than discovering more about the antique shop owner, she felt she knew even less about him than before.

Chapter Seventeen

Voices from the Past

The next day, Ziggy stayed home after Rosie's encounter with Sage and her wolfhound, Madigan, the day before. Rosie was disinclined to take her little dog to work with her, and the meeting had obviously put him off, too. He trotted off to his basket by the side of the range in the kitchen and snuggled down happily.

The weather remained gloomy; a solid sheet of cloud did not disperse and was only occasionally relieved somewhat by banks of mottled, mackerel-like clouds building up and rolling ominously over the glen. The occasional seagulls that followed the river into Erin's Glen flew around in a desultory fashion, mewing half-heartedly in the languid grey of the morning. Rosie felt exhausted and low in mood.

When she got to work, she opened the front door with her key. There was no sign of Father Asher. She sat down heavily in the office chair, sighing as she picked up letters to answer or file and worked through some phone calls to book various appointments into Father Asher's diary. A small note card fell out as she flicked through a bundle of letters. It had a picture of a fairy creature on the front. Rosie looked at it briefly and saw it was a brief confirmation from Sage of a meeting with Father Asher. The handwriting was distinctive, large and loopy. She recognised it from the handwritten leaflet the protestors had been handing out.

The priest was conspicuous by his absence. The office was silent, and the house seemed noticeably quiet. With a stab of regret and a sense of loss, she suddenly missed the old parish priest, whom she had worked with for decades, more keenly than ever. Father Gerard had a soothing confidence and faith that continually restored her flagging spirits during times like today. Usually, Rosie was happy to be left alone to get on with her duties, but today, she realised she felt lonely. She decided to do what usually cheered her up and make a nice pot of tea.

As she went through the house from the office into the back of the presbytery, she could hear Father Asher move about. So, he was here, after all. He was a bit of a mystery to Rosie. 'Ahh, leave him be', she thought to herself as she shrugged her shoulders and got on with her teamaking. As she moved about the large kitchen, she heard male voices talking out at the front. She quickly poured her tea, stirred in the milk and returned to the office to look out of the window at the front of the building where the voices were coming from. Father Asher was out there now, talking to Dan. Both looked serious; there was a low rumble of conversation. Rosie tried to be inconspicuous and sat at the desk just in front of the window. She made a show of typing on the computer keyboard but glanced up now and then, keeping her ears picked up for any snatches of words. Frustratingly, she couldn't make out exactly what they were saying, but she saw Father Asher return to the house, heard him come in the door and feigned mild surprise when he popped his head around the office door.

'I'm just popping out, Rosie. I've been busy at my desk upstairs. Lock up for me when you leave later, will you? I'm unsure how long I will be, but make sure the answering phone is switched on when you go.' Father Asher wriggled into his coat as he spoke and was out the door before Rosie could answer.

She waved out the window, but the two men didn't acknowledge her. Father Asher got into the police vehicle with Dan, and the white saloon car with a blue stripe down the side drove off, presumably to the station.

Rosie sat for a few minutes, musing on the implications of this. She had been unsettled by the priest's association with Sage from the community up by the fairy ring. Was there more to it than a mutual interest in preserving the beauty spot? Rosie's mind drifted off, considering what she knew about recent events, but a sense of frustration pervaded her thoughts. There was so much she didn't know.

Rosie jumped when the phone rang shrilly in the complete silence. Even the seagulls had given up the ghost today.

'Good morning, St Brigid's parish office. Rosie speaking. How may I help you?'

'Perfect telephone manner.' Rosie's heart warmed to hear Father Gerard's gentle, elderly tones.

'I was just thinking about you, Father!'

'Ah, I'm sure you were! You were always too nice to me, Rosie. I just thought I'd give you a ring and see how you are over there with all that shocking news there recently.'

'Oh, Father ––' Rosie was suddenly overcome with emotion. Not usually given to outbursts of tears, she could feel her eyes well up; the depth of her feelings surprised her. 'To be honest, I feel all at sea today. I was up at the fairy ring that morning and spoke to Dan. I don't know any details. He wouldn't tell me who it was that was found up there.

It's terrible to think some poor soul was lying dead up there all on their own. I don't know if it was foul play. I'm going to give Mary Jo a ring in a minute. I just thought I'd let her settle a bit from the shock.'

'Ah, right so. Yes, I'm sure she will appreciate a chat with you, Rosie; you two have always been such good friends. I'll get off the line, and you can give her a call. Or maybe you'll ring her on the mobile phone?' Rosie could imagine the twinkle in his eye as he asked this last question. Rosie's lack of skill in using the new type of phone was notorious, and in truth, she had quietly given up on it.

'Not today, Father, I'll stick to using the landline. But before I go, how are you keeping? How's life in Rocksheelan?'

Father Gerard had been moved to the parish of Rocksheelan recently. The bishop had referred to his 'ambiguous' position in the parish, which had angered Rosie, although she had tried to let it go. But all that was another story.

'Ah, grand, Rosie. It's done me good to have a change, and Erin's Glen has undoubtedly benefitted from having a younger man there with no history in the parish.'

Rosie doubted it but kept these thoughts to herself.

'I'll let you get on, Rosie. Give Mary Jo my regards, and it was lovely speaking with you.'

With that, Rosie heard the phone click as Father Gerard hung up. She held the phone to her ear for a few seconds; the flat, dull tone mirrored her mood that day, and despite the call from her old boss, she felt somewhat deflated.

She was about to put the phone down when she heard another click and then some vague whispering. She couldn't make out any words but could detect an urgent sound of hushed muttering. Another click, and it went dead, back to the monotonous tone of a disconnected line. Rosie sat for a few minutes looking at the phone in her hand and felt even more deeply unsettled. Perhaps she would dig out that unused mobile phone after all.

Chapter Eighteen

Invasion of Privacy

Earlier that afternoon, when Rosie had finished for the day at the parish office, she went straight home to a very appreciative Ziggy. Rosie gave him a perfunctory greeting and set about looking for her phone charger. She stood in the middle of her lounge, unsure where to look first, the dead mobile phone in her hand. Sighing, she returned the phone to her tweed coat pocket and made her call on the landline. She felt the need to speak with Mary Jo, and before she had even put the kettle on, she lifted the receiver and dialled the number for Mary Jo's home at Riverside House. Everything had sounded normal on the line, and Rosie waited patiently for an answer.

Rosie was relieved when she heard the comforting sound of Mary Jo's voice.

'Oh, I am so glad to hear from you! How are you doing?' Rosie asked her friend with concern.

There was silence on the other end of the phone, a silence heavy with the emotion of the day. Rosie heard Mary Jo take a deep breath.

'I'm doing alright, Rosie. Although it was a terrible shock.'

Rosie listened sympathetically and tried to soothe her friend. But in truth, she was keen to discover the details of Mary Jo's gruesome discovery.

The two old friends were accustomed to sharing secrets, and Mary Jo had no hesitation in sharing an in-depth description of how the body was arranged in the fairy ring.

'I'm no expert on these things, of course, but I would imagine that laying the body out in that way with symbols for each element sounds like some druid-like practice.'

Rosie tended to agree, 'Yes, this would show the perpetrator has some deeper symbolic intention to the murder, and it would indicate someone well-versed in these types of practices. It could be some Wiccan-type ceremony. Although, in truth, I don't really know about these things.'

'Right.' Mary Jo agreed, although not with much certainty. This was a little outside of her area of expertise, too.

They ended their call after a brief catch-up about more mundane matters at the school where Mary Jo worked, but the nun was still emotionally exhausted and was planning an early night. Rosie held the phone to her ear moments after they finished their conversation. She thought she heard a delayed click after Mary Jo put down the phone.

'Ah, for goodness' sake, you're getting paranoid in your old age!' Rosie chided herself. Ziggy was sitting, looking at her intently as if trying to hypnotise her.

'Alright, I get the hint. It's time for walkies!' Rosie pulled on her walking boots, grabbed Ziggy's lead, and was out the door again within a few minutes.

The walk with Ziggy gave Rosie a chance to reflect on her conversation with her friend and confidant. As Rosie strode along the familiar route on the streets close to where she lived, she felt increasingly uneasy. Her suspicions about the phones at the parish office and her home were unsettling. This device that connected her to the world was now fraught with suspicion. Rosie grappled with the disturbing notion that her private conversations were no longer private. A heavy weight of anxiety descended over her. As if trying to shake it off, she quickened her step – so much so that poor Ziggy had to run to keep up with her. Rosie's thoughts chased around her mind like a dog after its tail: why would someone want to tap the phones she used? Who in Erin's Glen would have the where-with-all to do something like that? It must be someone who was trying to keep a tab on what she was discussing.

With a stab of alarm, it dawned on her that the precise details of the body's nature had not yet been made public. No doubt, this was to preserve aspects of the case that only the perpetrator would know. She sincerely hoped her calls were, in fact, private. Rosie shook her head, feeling perplexed by recent events. She made a mental note not to discuss any theories she had about the murderer while on the phone. Usually, her number one confidant was Mary Jo, and they could easily meet in person, so that wouldn't be too much of a problem. Of course, there was always that mobile phone, too. She would make concerted efforts to find that charger.

The spring evening had cleared a little now, and the heavy bank of solid grey clouds was starting to break up. Some blue patches were becoming visible behind a few fluffy white clouds. The sun was low in the sky but added a weak yellow glimmer of warmth. Rosie felt a little brighter herself from the fresh air and the clear views of the hills and mountains surrounding Erin's Glen. Rosie could make out some white dots and hear the bleating of the lambs off in the distance. Rosie paused momentarily to admire the natural beauty of the scene in front of her. She followed the curve of the hills with her eyes and felt comforted by the soft lines of the landscape. Despite the recent trouble, Erin's Glen was a fine place to live. But as the sun sank lower in the sky, a chill began to creep in with the shadows.

'We'd best be getting home before dark.' Ziggy glanced up at her as if in agreement, and the two trotted back toward Rosie's bungalow. As the light changed and the temperature dipped, Rosie shivered. The bungalow was in sight, and her earlier unease was slowly starting to return. She hurried up the front path and paused by the front door. She lingered there momentarily; a perfumed scent hung about the small porchway by the front door. Rosie felt that she recognised it but was unsure where it was from. She put the key in the door, and, following the dictates of her intuition, she moved inside slowly. Distracted by the unexpected perfume and her uneasy feelings, she picked up some junk mail and placed it on the table by the door. She stood in the hall while Ziggy sat down, eyeing her curiously. Ziggy glanced from side to side and gave a little bark. He began to shiver slightly and looked ill at ease himself.

Rosie took note of her little dog's visceral reactions. The responses of her four-legged friend were often more dependable than those of humans. His were immediate, raw and uncensored by reason. His look of unease and shaking body unnerved Rosie. She murmured to him in a comforting manner as she unclipped his lead. Usually, he was off like a shot to his food bowl or basket when they got back from a walk, but today, he nuzzled into her, in no hurry to scamper off. She sensed he needed to feel her physical presence and was glad of his reassuring company. She crouched down with him for a moment, and after a comforting pat on the head, she slowly got up and peered down the hallway. As she crept through her home, glancing into each room as she made her way along the hall, fifty percent of her scolded herself for her silly suspicions, and the other fifty percent felt very uneasy. She had a strong, unsubstantiated feeling that someone had been in her house. Nothing was disturbed. No drawers or cupboard doors left open. There was no sign of a broken window or door forced open. Materially, everything looked as it did when she left earlier. But it felt different. She knew that Ziggy sensed it, too.

After she had checked out each room, she felt a little more comfortable. She put the kettle on and scrapped some food onto Ziggy's dish. These familiar routines comforted her, and she returned to the living room with her cup of tea. She looked around for the mobile phone. She couldn't see it anywhere. Just where had she put it? Despite her frustration, she felt less anxious. However, Rosie's confidence was short-lived. Suddenly, she heard the gate to her garden creak loudly. Rosie braced herself.

Chapter Nineteen

School Days

'**G**ood morning, Mr Quninnnn....'

The class of seven-year-olds intoned as a group, trailing off the end of the antique shop owner's name as all groups of seven-year-olds seem to do.

Cornelius Quinn stood in front of the class alongside Miss Mulligan, the Class Teacher. The young woman wore a bright blue pinafore dress and a multicoloured striped jumper. She had a broad smile, and her hands were clasped in front of her. Her blond curls bounced as she spoke, 'Thank you for agreeing to come in to talk to us today. Mr Quinn, Class Two is very excited to have you here with us today – *Billy!*'

Miss Mulligan changed her tone quickly as she stared at a red-haired boy at the back who was pulling faces at a stoic-looking girl next to him.

Cornelius looked around at the twenty or so excited seven-year-olds; he reckoned most of them got very enthusiastic about most things. He smiled uncertainly as the sea of expectant faces looked at him.

Miss Mulligan placed a worryingly small chair in front of the group. 'Make yourself comfortable, Mr Quinn,' the young teacher grinned at him. Cornelius sat down gingerly on the low chair. He was genuinely concerned he might not get up again, but he was aware of a ripple of distraction that ran through the group. Seven-year-olds have a limited attention span, and he realised he needed to get on quickly before Class Two's mercurial attention was lost.

'Right then, good morning, Class Two. Does anyone know why I am here this morning?'

Silence.

'Right, well...' he trailed off, uncertain where to start.

The teacher stepped in, 'Now, Class Two, we have talked about this; Mr Quinn is here to tell us all about the fairies. Many of you had questions about the little people, and I am no expert---' Miss Mulligan laughed lightly and, as an aside to Cornelius, explained, *'I'm from Dublin.'*

He nodded. A girl from the city wouldn't know about such matters.

She turned back to the class and raised her voice slightly, smiling at the rows of little faces. 'Many of you have been listening to the local news about the hill fort, so we have asked Mr Quinn here to come in to tell you all about the fairies. He has read lots of old books and is our local folklore expert.' Miss Mulligan smiled encouragingly and retreated to her desk chair. A high-backed leather one, Cornelius noted with envy.

He turned back to the class, 'Well, the fairy people have been here a long time. Does anyone know their real Irish name?

The girl with the pigtails shot her hand up right away. *'Aoes-si'*

'Well done, that's correct, young lady. I shall refer to them as *"the Shee"*. Do you know we have many different types of fairies? The main three types are the land fairies, the fairies of the air, and *the dark fairies*.'

Miss Mulligan looked a bit alarmed.

'But we won't talk about the dark ones today.' He added quickly.

He glanced reassuringly at Miss Mulligan; she visibly relaxed.

Cornelius went on to explain how the fairies of the land were ancient creatures who looked after nature. They were custodians of the land, bogs, mountains, hills, and fields.

Miss Mulligan had pinned up a picture of a delicate, feminine-looking fairy with gossamer wings dressed in a floaty pink costume. It looked like an image from a Victorian English fairytale picture book.

Cornelius pointed to it, 'Do you see this creature here? Well, I can tell you the *Shee* looks nothing like that. '

The class teacher looked a bit crestfallen.

'What do they look like, Mister?' Billy called out from the back.

'Like you.'

The class laughed. Billy swiped at the boy nearest to him, who was smirking and pointing at Billy.

'*Billy!*' Miss Mulligan interjected.

The serious girl with the pigtails was sitting patiently with her hand up.

'Roisin,' Miss Mulligan called to her, indicating she could ask the next question.

'Mr Quinn, have you ever seen the *Shee*?' Roisin looked at Mr Quinn earnestly.

'Ah now, sure, I've seen plenty.' The class listened intently. 'And they do indeed look like us. They love dancing and singing and playing harps.'

'How do they live…like what do they eat?' A big boy with a mop of chestnut brown hair cut into a bowl shape asked.

'They are great hunters. They are out at night on their little horses, hunting for food. They live off the land and have a grand life – eating, singing, dancing – just grand.'

Many children in the class were nodding in agreement.

'Is anyone here frightened of the *Shee*?' No one raised their hand; some shook their head confidently, unwilling to admit any fear. Miss Mulligan opened her eyes wide and arched her eyebrows in dramatic mock disbelief.

'Ah now, there might have been a few who have been having bad dreams, Mr Quinn.' She confirmed, smiling at the class visitor. Behind her hand, she whispered, '*Especially* after the recent news.'

He nodded in understanding and looked back at the children, 'Well, now there is nothing to be fearful of. You don't bother them, and they won't bother you.' Cornelius grinned at the youngsters, who looked back at him thoughtfully.

'So, Mr Quinn, do the *Shee* live in the fort?' A small girl at the front asked.

'Yes, they do indeed. The Celts drove them into the fort, and they have stayed there to this day. So, as I say, you don't bother them; they won't bother you. There's no need to go to the fort looking for them. It's best to stay away.' He looked around at all the little faces, keen to get his point across.

'Right, well, thanks very much, Mr Quinn.' Miss Mulligan sprang to her feet and stood beside him as he slowly unbent from the little chair.

'And before I go....' Cornelius took out a small pouch from his inside pocket.

'Some fairy dust for you all...' relishing a parting dramatic flourish, he threw its contents around lavishly. The children put their hands up to catch the glittering sprinkles with yelps of delight. Miss Mulligan stood looking less impressed by the shower of glitter that had littered her classroom and glinted off the children's hair and school uniforms.

'This'll take some explaining to the cleaner and the parents.' she thought.

Cornelius was swiftly guided to the door and ushered out to the school reception area.

***

Later that day, after the school bell announced the end of the day and the children had all left, Miss Mulligan went to the staff room for a strong coffee to keep her going until she, too, could go home.

'How did the visit go?' Mr Corrigan, the headteacher, called over.

'Ah, just grand, thanks.' Miss Mulligan sat down heavily. Her friend, Mrs Kane, the Class Three Teacher, perched beside her.

'*He* might be fooled, but I'm not.' Mrs Kane nodded at the retreating back of the headteacher as he returned to his office. 'What happened?' she pressed.

Miss Mulligan hesitated. She had thought it would be a good idea to ask a local expert on Irish folklore to talk to the class. Some children had been unsettled about the proposed tourist centre, and this had been magnified after the body was found. The teacher had hoped he could allay their fears.

'Well, honestly, all he did was create a mess with glitter in my classroom and tell them not to go near the hill fort.

Mrs Kane pulled her mouth down at each side. 'Not particularly helpful'

'It wasn't.' Miss Mulligan confirmed. In fact, she had felt unsettled by his keenness to keep people away from the fort.

'Now, why would that be?' she thought to herself.

Chapter Twenty

Mysterious Disappearances

Dan had felt increasingly unsettled about Toddy. Dan had visited the cottage and intended to speak with Toddy, but Toddy was not there. Toddy's absence had niggled him.

The seasoned guard had spent a few frustrating shifts at the police station, filling in endless reports and forms detailing what had been found on the fairy ring. His superiors were slow to send backups, and Dan felt a familiar sense of isolation in the small backwater of Erin's Glen.

After a few hours at his desk, he pushed away from his paperwork, rubbed his eyes, stretched, and decided to go out and do some proper detective work.

Sergeant Kennedy had returned to the station and seemed preoccupied with his own paperwork. He barely looked at Dan as the older man picked up his coat and a torch. 'I'll see you in an hour or so, Sergeant.'

Sergeant Kennedy grunted by way of a reply, and Dan made his way out into the fresh spring air. It was dusk, and Dan knew he needed to move quickly to pursue his line of enquiry before dark settled in. He hesitated as he approached the police car and, after a moment's consideration, decided to hop on his bike instead. He had good lights, and it would draw less attention to his presence.

Dan enjoyed the gentle physical exertion as he peddled along the street. The movement and fresh air were a welcome contrast to being constrained in his office chair all day in the fusty interior of the police station.

The rhythmic push on the pedals helped him settle into a more meditative state. As he cycled along the familiar route, he mulled over the murder of Gerry Macauley. He was sure Toddy was involved somehow. Toddy was a man with a problematic past. He was isolated, eccentric and poor. But was he a murderer? Dan could remember Toddy's parents: an indulgent, over-protective mother and a big bully of a father who was too fond of the sauce. As a young police officer, Dan had reason to have words with Toddy's father on several occasions due to his unruly behaviour after a few jars in The Thatch bar. However, despite his father's shortcomings, Toddy was extremely attached to him and appeared to be devastated when his parents passed away.

Dan reached the fairy ring in a few minutes. The twilight sky was now streaked with dark ribbons of heavy cloud. The earlier pink glow of the late afternoon was starting to fade fast. The police officer came to a halt by the sign that indicated Erin's Glen Woods and pushed his bicycle along the rough dirt path that circled through the forest up to the fort. As Dan pushed his bike along, he was aware of his breath in the cold night air. The chill of the early evening created a crystal-like clarity, and every sound seemed amplified. The gravel crunched under his boots as he plodded along uphill. The late afternoon din of the sparrows fussing with each other had now subsided and was replaced by the haunting hoot of an owl calling out across the woods. Dan stopped and pulled up the collar of his jacket. He looked up towards the fairy ring. Its iconic tree was silhouetted on top, its bare branches in dark contrast to the star-studded backdrop. A few wisps of gold and pink still streaked across the dome of the night sky, and even Dan, a seasoned officer with a lot on his mind, was touched by its cosmic beauty.

At this point, he was at a fork in the road. He took the path that led down to Toddy's house. He had knocked at his door earlier that day, but Toddy was not there. Dan was keen to speak with him, but it would be informal. He didn't want to spook the vulnerable man. He'd tell Toddy it was a welfare check to make sure he was coping alright after the shock of the news. It would only be natural for Toddy to feel unsettled with a probable murder happening so close by anyway.

As Dan carried on his way, he could make out the outline of the cottage, black against the stark trees. There were no lights on inside the house, but Dan knew Toddy lived his nocturnal life in candlelight, so he was not concerned about the seeming darkness inside the cottage. Dan's eyes had adjusted to the lack of light as evening settled in. He continued down the rough dirt path through the trees, keeping the cottage in view. Stray twigs and brambles pulled at the spokes in his bike wheels, and he cursed mildly as he stopped to free one up. He thought that he heard a crack behind him. He paused. *It's probably just a small woodland animal.* The experienced police officer chastised himself for letting his imagination get the better of him. Just then, the police phone he carried buzzed, indicating a call was coming in.

'Dan, it's Kennedy here. This could mean something or nothing, but I've just had a call come in from Sam Bazley's wife. She's reported him missing. So, keep an eye out and your ears open. Could it just be an unrelated domestic, or perhaps it is related to all this business with the body.'

Dan acknowledged the message with a terse, 'Aye. Will do. See you later.' and finished the call. He was keen to get on and see what was going on with Toddy. He dropped his bike on its side as he approached the cottage. There was no sign of life, no flickering candlelight inside, and no smoke from the chimney.

Dan hesitated by the front door. He wanted to check on Toddy, but it wasn't an official search. He tried the front door handle. It was locked, although the lock was flimsy. He knocked loudly. No answer. Dan crept around the cottage. He flashed his torch through the window and swept it around the chaotic living room and kitchen. The usual debris of books, newspapers, food cartons, bottles, cans and the remains of a meal littered the table and surfaces. The guard made one more sweep around with the torch and did a double take. Dan fixed the light on a chair by the table. Over the chair was draped a high-visibility jacket. The sort of jacket a builder would wear. Dan leaned closer to look. He squinted as he made out the logo on the jacket: *S.B. Builders.* Now, what did that mean? Dan needed to get onto his sergeant and find out more.

Where was Sam, and why was his jacket in Toddy's house? Where was Toddy? The house was empty. As this was an unofficial visit, Dan had to abandon this last question and return to the station.

Chapter Twenty-One

Haunted

The previous night, Toddy had been in a state. The evenings were the worst for him. During daylight hours, Toddy kept himself occupied outside and only returned home when the darkness crept in. But he had been up on the fairy ring most evenings during twilight, keeping watch as a crepuscular redness bled into the night sky. Most evenings, the cold and dark forced him back inside the squalid home. But, after his recent experience out on the road back from town late at night, he avoided heading to the pub and instead sat indoors, alone. Bad things were happening in Erin's Glen, and he knew the local people would blame him.

He had tried to make friends. But people didn't stay. Once they got to know him, they backed off. He had made a new friend recently, but he had gone too. Toddy tried to do what was asked of him, but he was still left alone. People made no sense to him. He decided that he would have nothing to do with them from now on. He had done everything, and he was still tortured.

A clench of fear, dread and regret knotted in his stomach. He couldn't eat. The knot filled him so much he could hardly breathe. His breathing was shallow and rapid. When he tried to fill his lungs, he couldn't. The panic just got worse. He felt like he was drowning in his fear.

Tonight, he sat vigil by the empty fireplace, too frightened to go into the room he usually slept in. The shame of his fear ate away at him. A grown man, frightened of what? A few shadows and knocks around the place. He tried to dismiss his anxieties and rationalise what he saw and heard. But the unease just kept building. Tonight was worse than ever.

He stood up from the worn chair by the fireplace and caught sight of his long, pale face in the cracked and spotted mirror on the wall opposite. A photograph of his father, Tommy, as a little boy, was on the mantle. He looked into the black-and-white image of his younger father standing by the gate of this very cottage. His father's image seemed to mock him. His daddy had grown up in this tiny house with nine siblings and his two parents. At one time, this cottage was bursting at the seams with unruly children and preoccupied adults. His grandparents, too, were busy from dawn to dusk with work and chores. A considerable effort was needed to keep body and soul together. There was constant noise and activity, not like now.

Now, he was all alone. He was the son and heir of the legacy he had been given, a legacy he had tried to nurture and protect but had failed. He studied his shadowy face in the gloom, a flickering candle the only illumination.

'Look at ya, a disgrace.' He derided his reflection, filled with self-loathing and disgust. Standing by the mantle, he folded his hands on the familiar iron of the fireplace and rested his head. He felt so weary and alone. He could almost sleep like this, like the horses in the fields standing in the night. Suddenly, a low rumbling noise in the chimney made him jump. In a split second, his lethargy was eradicated, and all his senses were alert. He stepped back from the chimney, looking at it in horror. Sounds of scratching and dragging kept his attention focused as he stood now in the middle of the cluttered room, his eyes wide with a wild, fearful curiosity. 'What in God's name was that?' He whispered to himself. He stood transfixed, hardly daring to breathe.

Silence.

He strained his ears as he slowly approached the chimney. After a few seconds of quiet, he felt brave enough to put his ear to the wall beside the fireplace.

Nothing.

Toddy's rapid, thudding heartbeat began to settle to a steadier rhythm. He sat down again in the chair, feeling heavy with dread and abject fear. The cottage was quiet again. Some wind rustled the branches of the trees outside, and he could feel a cool breeze brush past his cheek. He reminded himself to fix a crack in the window tomorrow. But then he'd thought that every night recently, and he hadn't done anything about it the next day. His head felt like it was stuffed with cotton wool recently. His stomach lurched about in anxious knots. A familiar wave of nausea crept up from his belly.

'Get a grip, man,' he scolded himself. But as he stood in the middle of the untidy room, his hands balled into fists, he looked around, unsure what to do next.

He picked up a bundle of handwritten notes by the side of his chair and leafed through them. He wasn't a great reader but understood what they instructed him to do. He had tried, but he knew he had failed. Why were they still making his life such a nightmare? He threw the notes down on the floor in frustration and despair.

He could hear the wind whipping up outside. It began to screech and keen around the corners of the cottage. He put his hands over his ears to block it out. After a few seconds, Toddy closed his eyes and opened them, realising he was now in complete darkness.

The candle had been blown out. Toddy looked around slowly, the familiar piles of books and items taking on ominous shapes. He could make out the whites of his eyes set in his grey face reflected in the old mirror. He rolled his eyes around, adjusting to the darkness. The small crescent moon provided a slither of light that slanted across the room. He slowly took his hands away from his ears and surveyed his living space. The thin band of moonlight illuminated the smooth wood of a worn chair seat, an expanse of the mahogany table and an old trunk. The silver light exposed a broad line that seemed to glow in the darkness. The dust had settled on the highlighted surfaces. But the fine dusting of powder had been disturbed.

Toddy could make out some footprints that made him gasp in horror. Small, hooflike prints marched over the chair seat, across the table, along the top of the trunk and off in the direction of his bedroom. He felt paralysed with fear. His mind conjured up all manner of images of the non-human creature that must have made those preternatural prints.

As he stood transfixed to the spot, frozen, the chimney shuddered and belched, and a scattering of something rushed into the grate. He couldn't see what it was. And he didn't stop to look. He ran to the cottage door and fumbled at the old handle that always stuck, petrified that he would be unable to escape. He needed to get away. He needed to escape the memories, the voices and whatever it was that was torturing him with recriminations.

He grabbed his old rucksack, which had a tin mug and pot hanging from it, strung his spare boots over his shoulder and made for the door.

The door jammed.

He twisted and pulled at the handle, panic-stricken. At last, it gave way and let him free. He ran off into the night. The door banged shut behind him, forced closed by the strong gust of wind that was now full force on the cottage. He scrambled up the dirt path, away from the cottage, away from the fairy ring, and off into the darkness beyond.

Chapter Twenty-Two

Father's Confessions

The following week, Rosie was at work, busy filing letters and completing entries in the parish records, when she decided to pop into Quinn's Curiosities later that same day. She was still unsure about Cornelius Quinn. Perhaps there was more to the dapper antique shop owner than met the eye. Rosie knew from experience that appearances could be very deceptive, so she decided to get to know Cornelius better and learn more.

She sat for a moment and let her mind drift back to the Quinn family of old. She could recall the young Cornelius and his brother. Now, what was his brother's name? She couldn't remember but knew it would come to her later. Rosie let her gaze drift outside and looked up at the sky, frowning, trying to dredge up memories from the past. They were a very academic family. The mother had taught the piano. She gave lessons in the family home. The father had taught Latin at the boys' school. Rosie herself had gone to the girl's convent school and had little to do with the academic Quinn boys, so Cornelius and his brother were not well known to her. The brother had gone off to university in England. Now, what was it he went off to study? Ah yes, she remembered her mother telling her. He studied Celtic Antiquities. Strange, he never came back. Undoubtedly, he would have been interested in the fairy ring's history. Her memories of Cordelia were fuzzy. Rosie remembered Cordelia as musical and creative. However, Rosie played no instruments, so their paths didn't cross very much.

Rosie shook herself out of her trip down memory lane and eyed the open drawer of the filing cabinet. 'Right, these letters aren't going to file themselves.' Taking herself in hand, she began leafing through the papers on her desk. She glanced at her watch. She needed to make some headway; otherwise, she'd be late getting away today and wanted to visit Quinn's antique shop before it closed. So, keen to get on with her routine jobs, Rosie's heart sank when Father Asher tapped the office door and appeared with a pile of ring binders.

'Ah, Rosie, good morning.' The priest greeted her warmly.

Rosie replied distractedly, 'Father,' as she peered into a deep drawer full of filed letters.

Father Asher sat down, plonking the heavy binders onto the desk. He waited until she sat upright and peered back at him over her thick spectacles.

'Can I help you, Father?'

'Rosie, I need to get these accounts all up to date. It seems that the police are interested in the parish accounts.' Father Asher paused and cleared his throat. He shrugged and grinned as he continued, 'They want to clear me from any connection with the situation up at the hill fort. It seems my ideas on saving the planet have got me into some trouble. It would also seem that they think I might have some financial motive, too.'

Rosie blinked blankly at him, taking in what he was saying.

Father Asher sat quietly for a moment, running his fingers along the edge of a binder. He suddenly looked downcast. Rosie felt sorry for this young man who seemed to have gotten involved in a situation out of his depth.

'It's not been a perfect start to my career, I'm afraid. Bishop Branagh is none too happy with me, I can tell you.'

Rosie frowned and looked earnestly at him.

The priest continued, 'Well, people in the town have been discussing my involvement with Sage.'

Rosie sat quietly and listened.

'I feel passionately about God's earth. It's scandalous how people are treating it. It would be a desecration to build on that ancient site, no matter one's religious beliefs.' The juvenile cleric looked appealingly at Rosie. 'But my passionate opinions about the environment would never push me to violence.' Father Asher shook his head firmly, conveying the depth of his feelings.

Rosie decided to seize the moment. This was the first time Father Asher had sat with her to talk properly. She was suddenly overcome by maternal sympathy for this young man with no family nearby. She was also curious.

'Tell me, Father, what is the story with Sage? Who is she, and why is she here?'

Father Asher hesitated. He looked down at his hands fanned out before him and sighed. 'Well, I know she is from the city. She feels very strongly about the erosion of the natural environment and feels that Ireland is selling herself out to attract tourists. That's why Sage and her group are so much against the building of this tourist centre. I suppose that's why I have become friends with Sage. We disagree on points of faith and belief, but we both feel deeply about the earth.' Father Asher paused here, looking off into the far distance. He continued, 'Also, I suppose I thought I might see if I could persuade her and at least some of her group to attend church. I hoped she would see how we have much in common despite superficial appearances.'

Rosie doubted that, but she said nothing for a moment. She had a sense that the priest knew more. Rosie noted how every word he uttered seemed well-considered. Equally, she reined in her usual effusiveness and thought carefully about the questions she asked the young man in front of her.

After a few seconds of silence, she asked, 'But was Sage involved in the murder of Gerry Macauley, do you think?'

'I don't know, Rosie; what I do know is that Gerry's body was laid out in some fashion that has made the police think that she or some of her group have somehow been involved. I don't know the details. I admit Sage has strongly held beliefs. I suppose it *could* be possible. The police seem to think so.' Father Asher hesitated again. 'In fact...' The priest paused and shuffled about on his seat. Rosie waited. '...in confidence, I know I can trust you, Rosie.'

He looked at her. Rosie confirmed that he could trust her with a decisive nod.

'Well, it would seem Gerry had a note from Sage in his pocket. The note invited him up to the hill fort to talk with her. I haven't seen it, but it said she could meet him to discuss the plans if he cared to come up to the fairy ring. The date she suggested was the night he died. This doesn't look good for Sage, but she has witnesses who say she was with her group at their campsite by Slievecairn, so she wasn't at the fairy ring that night. But the police don't see her group members as credible witnesses. Sage has been told not to leave Erin's Glen until all this has been resolved. For that matter, *I've* been told to stay in the parish, too. You can imagine how that has gone down with the bishop! Anyway, sorry. Enough about my troubles. We need to get these financial records up to date. How are you with spreadsheets?' Father Asher smiled hopefully at Rosie.

'Leave them with me.' Rosie patted the binders and grinned back at him reassuringly. Her heart had sunk, and a feeling of powerlessness swept over her. But the last thing this poor man needed was for her to unburden her self-doubt to him concerning her lack of IT skills. In addition to her doubt about the spreadsheets, she felt doubtful about him. Rosie had a strong feeling that the priest had got himself into something more than he bargained for – and that he wasn't being entirely upfront with her.

Father Asher's usual jovial manner returned. He stood up and clapped his hands, rubbing them enthusiastically. 'Ah, that's just grand Rosie; I knew I could depend on you.' She nodded back at him and smiled. The moment of intense sharing had now passed, and Father Asher was returning to his usual cheery demeanour. He bounded out of the room.

Rosie pulled out the Yellow Pages as the office door closed behind him. She scanned the business phone directory to find the telephone number for Quinn's Curiosities. She dialled the number, and it clicked on the answering machine at once. Rosie put the phone down. She hated talking to those machines and usually got muddled up. 'Why is nothing straightforward?' she mumbled to herself. She would have to go around there later unannounced and throw herself on the mercy of Cornelius Quinn.

CHAPTER TWENTY-THREE

Paper Trails

Behind the scenes, Sergeant Kennedy and Dan were both slumped over a large desk at the local police station. They had just returned from a visit to Sam's house with two large boxes filled with papers relating to Sam's business. The builder had been located and was told to remain within a fifty-mile radius of Erin's Glen. The two unopened boxes stood mutely between the police officers. Dan was the first to start opening one, delving into the contents, pulling out papers randomly, and giving each document a cursory glance.

Dan pulled out the papers, stopped, and looked more closely at plans for another building up at the hill fort. Attached to it was an unsigned agreement between Sam and Sage. Dan passed it to his boss, who looked at it briefly and nodded.

'Yes, I'm convinced he has something to do with this.' Sergeant Kennedy pronounced sullenly, 'Sam Bazley is up to no good. He's always been trouble and always will be. It was only a matter of time until he got himself into some serious trouble.'

Sergeant Kennedy sat down, watching Dan as he continued sorting through handfuls of papers of assorted sizes. Dan didn't respond to his superior's less-than-professional description of Sam.

The senior police officer was on a roll, '*And* we have testimony from that wee girl, Deirdre, to say she saw Sam and Gerry fighting on the street.' Dan looked at his Sergeant and raised one eyebrow. Sergeant Kennedy relented. 'Well, alright, maybe not *fighting* as such, but they *were* arguing. What were they arguing about? That's what I want to know. I reckon Sam got hold of him again ... that's it, Sam and Sage lured Gerry up to the hill fort and killed him there.'

'How?' Dan fixed his boss with a steady gaze...although that empty bottle of medication was found in Gerry's pocket...' Dan trailed off. This detail bothered him.

Sergeant Kennedy was dismissive, 'Sure, that was just his allergy medication.'

'So how exactly did Sam kill Gerry?' Dan looked at his boss with an aggressive stare.

Sergeant Kennedy clamped his mouth shut, and after a few seconds, he continued, 'Well, I don't know yet. But I'm sure Sam was responsible for it – him and that hippy woman. They are in cahoots. Wanting to build their own centre by the looks of things, ' Kennedy nodded at the document Dan had unearthed. 'I'm convinced he took himself off after Gerry was found to try to avoid us, and sure, *she* speaks to no one.' Kennedy paused here, considering Sage's role in recent events.

Dan waited, keeping his gaze fixed on his boss.

The sergeant finished by mustering more conviction and booming, 'It's only a matter of time until we get to the bottom of this, and we'll see Sam and that cult leader woman behind bars.'

Dan wasn't so sure and was keen to change the conversation, so he asked, 'What about the widow?'

'Mrs MacAulay?' Kennedy looked at Dan quizzically.

'Yes, what is she set to gain from her husband's death?' Dan queried.

Kennedy laughed hollowly, 'A huge mortgage and a second-hand Audi. Not enough to do her husband in for. No, I've already looked into all that. Gerry's insurance only covers a big funeral. He obviously wanted a good send-off. Other than that, nothing. In fact, Aisling Macauley won't be able to afford to keep that house on her bookkeeper's salary. As my mother would have said, Gerry was all "fur coat and no knickers": he had a fancy house on a bank loan but no money to speak of. Aisling would have been better off with Gerry alive and well.'

Kennedy was sitting looking into the far distance, mulling over the details of Gerry's financial situation. He cleared his throat and leaned over towards his colleague. 'Sure, you must remember that Gerry fancied himself a stockbroker a few years ago. He even started dressing in one of those stripy shirts and braces. He looked a sight!'

Dan nodded with a small smile. He recalled how the locals giggled and nudged each other when Gerry paraded up and down Rainbow Row in his showy suit and tie. Satisfied with Dan's memory of events, Kennedy continued, 'Well, apparently, he lost all his money. He had to get the house re-mortgaged. That poor wee woman has stood by him all these years.'

Dan returned to the shifting mound of papers he had begun searching through. Some were small handwritten chits for work done and money received. Some were barely legible, thin paper slips from credit card payments. Dan peered at each one in turn.

Paperwork was not Sam's strong point. How did Sam ever make sense of all this for his taxes? What a mess. Dan shook his head and carried on. He methodically made three piles. One was of definite interest, one contained items that *might* be significant, and a third was irrelevant bits and pieces. Dan noted a child's drawings, presumably from Sam's young son. Dan had no children himself. It was a source of pain for him and his wife but one they had learned to live with over the years.

Sergeant Kennedy sighed deeply, and he looked at his watch. Dan could tell his boss's interest in the case was waning. Kennedy would love to get this all wrapped up and tidied away. His superior's theories were that someone had found Gerry's body and decided to lay him out or that Sam and Sage were behind it. But Dan was sure it was not just a case of some nutter finding a body and laying it out with all the stones and flowers and whatnot. Nor did he think Sam would be stupid enough to kill Gerry. Dan was convinced there was more to it. He would find out what really had happened to Gerry Macauley. Unfortunately, that meant getting on with boring jobs like this one.

The sergeant was restless. After studying the document Dan had handed him earlier, he stood up, sighed and announced, 'I need to make a phone call home.'

'Okay.' Dan responded, distracted by the paperwork in front of him as his boss left the room. As he sifted through the papers, his mind returned to Toddy. Where was he, and why had he bolted? Kennedy was quick enough to put an alert out for Sam when he was reported missing by his wife but not so quick to do it for Toddy. It turned out that Sam's "disappearance" was just a misunderstanding. Sam was visiting a construction site down south and decided to stay over. The drink was flowing. He'd got blutered and forgot to ring his wife to let her know. Given recent events, Sam's wife, Cathy, was worried and contacted the police. Kennedy had responded immediately, seeing it as a sign of Sam's guilt.

But his boss had dismissed Dan's concerns about Toddy without even considering the implications. Instead, Kennedy had focused on Sam's jacket being in Toddy's house. As far as Kennedy was concerned, this brought Sam closer to the scene, and the fact that Sam had seemingly disappeared meant Sam had something to hide – in Kennedy's mind, at least. Dan let these details roll around in his mind without trying to make any firm conclusions.

Dan was well aware of the town gossip, mainly fuelled by Mrs Blaney, the owner of the local B&B. She had never liked Sam and was only too quick to spread rumours about him. Dan stopped for a moment and thought back to the reasons why Mrs Blaney disliked Sam so much. He wasn't sure why. What he did know was that Kennedy seemed to have it in for Sam. The builder was just a bit younger than his boss, Sergeant Kennedy. Dan knew there had been a rivalry between them, probably going back to their school days. Sergeant Kennedy was forever making remarks about how well Sam was doing for himself. These comments were usually made with a sarcastic tone. Dan could see that Sam's newly built five-bedroomed house set in a vast garden contrasted sharply with the modest terrace that his boss lived in with his wife and young family.

Dan continued to grab out handfuls of sheets of invoices, building plans, letters and planning applications. His head throbbed from the mental effort of concentrating on each piece of paper in case one document could lead to the killer. If there even *was* a killer. The lack of firm substance frustrated the seasoned officer. It was all so slippery. And all this nonsense about the *Shee* wasn't helping either.

Dan's eye rested again on the document he had shown his boss earlier. Now, what was all that about? He was about to pick it up again to consider it when the bell at the station's front desk rang.

Glad of a break from his laborious task, Dan lumbered out stiffly to the front desk.

He stopped when he saw who it was. His complicated day was about to get even more complicated.

Chapter Twenty-Four

Technology Old and New

When Rosie finished work for the afternoon, she headed straight to Quinn's Curiosities to find Cornelius Quinn there. She wanted to uncover the mysteries of spreadsheets and shed more light on the other mysteries in Erin's Glen – including him.

She had just parked the Mini along Rainbow Row and was locking the door when she noticed Mrs Blaney and Mrs Kirkpatrick standing opposite the police station. They were glancing over at the station and discussing something of immediate interest.

'Hello there, ladies!' Rosie trotted over briskly, keen to find out what was attracting their attention.

'Oh, hello, Rosie.' Mrs Kirkpatrick smiled warmly while Mrs Blaney, the more ruthless of the two, kept her eyes fixed on the police station entrance.

'Any news then?' Rosie nodded in the direction of their gaze.

Mrs Blaney enthusiastically spun around, 'Well, Rosie, it's all been going on. I was telling Mrs Kirkpatrick here all about the goings on concerning Sam Bazley––'

'Well, *I* was telling *you*.' Mrs Kirkpatrick interrupted, correcting her friend.

Mrs Blaney glared back at her and, after a split-second pause, carried on, 'And guess what?'

Rosie did not have a chance to respond as Mrs Blaney continued, 'He's just been arrested.'

'Arrested? How do you know?' Rosie queried.

'He's just been taken into the station, over there.'

Mrs Kirpatrick interjected, 'Well, he's just gone in himself, like.'

Keen to share her part in the drama, Mrs Blaney couldn't resist adding, 'Of course, it's all due to my tip-off. I was in there half an hour ago. I told Dan to get Sam in for questioning.'

Rosie looked at her. 'And why would that be then?' she queried.

'I couldn't possibly say...' Mrs Blaney looked past Rosie. Fixing her eyes on the station, she shut her mouth.

The three women gazed at the building as if it were about to reveal a secret. Rosie was the first to break the spell. 'Well, we'll see what's what, I suppose. I need to get on.'

'Right-o.' The other two women chorused as they continued to stand vigil on the pavement, keeping their eyes fixed on the police station.

Rosie fixed *her* eyes on Quinn's Curiosities, took a deep breath, and marched over to the shop, determined to learn more about spreadsheets and Cornelius Quinn. Putting her hand in her pocket, she realised her mobile phone was in there, useless thing, she thought to herself.

The light was fading, bringing the day to a close, but a soft glow emanated from the shop window. The shop sign above the door swayed and creaked gently in the chilly breeze that swept along the street.

As Rosie opened the door and entered the shop's interior, it felt like she was stepping back into days gone by. A multitude of old clocks ticked loudly in the peaceful atmosphere of the store, and Rosie suddenly felt very conscious of time itself. A colossal sideboard, chairs with chunky legs and a massive table with leaves folded down dominated the inside of the shop. The walls were covered with paintings set in ornate gilt frames and old rugs in rich ruby red and gold hues. The shelves were filled with carefully arranged china, pewter and silverware items. Rosie scanned the shop, taking in the magnificent array of antiques.

'Good afternoon, Rosie. What a delight to see you again.' Cornelius' face creased into a broad smile, his blue eyes twinkling. 'How may I help you?'

'Cosmos!' Rosie blurted out.

'Sorry?' the antique shop owner looked puzzled.

'Your brother. I was trying to think of his name earlier, and it just popped into my head. Sorry Cornelius. I remember faces and pictures like photos, but names sometimes elude me! I knew it would come back to me eventually. Sorry about that!'

'Ah, I see, Rosie. The same thing happens to me, although I don't have the photographic memory for faces and pictures as you do. Yes, Cosmos. Cosmos is the clever one in the family.'

Rosie was about to interrupt, her mouth forming a small 'o' shape. Cornelius caught this and, pre-empting her protest at his self-deprecation, continued:

'I might have got a bachelor's degree in history, but Cosmos is the *real* academic in the family. He is a Professor of Celtic Antiquity at Oxford. He is an amazing man. My nephew, Hayden, is extremely interested in the topic himself but has decided to take a 'gap year', as all the young people seem to do nowadays. Hayden is visiting Erin's Glen at the moment. I believe you met my nephew recently?'

Rosie nodded, warming to the subject of Cornelius' family background. 'So, it runs in the family, then?' Cornelius looked back at her blankly.

'Antiquities, history.' Rosie threw her hands around at the displayed aged artefacts to show her meaning.

'Ah yes, of course. Indeed. Yes, we are all that way inclined. Hayden has been spending time here in Erin's Glen because he is fascinated by its rich history and the fairy ring. He's––'

Cornelius stopped abruptly, suddenly aware of Rosie's intense concentration on his words. He put a finger to his lips and paused, a small smile playing at the edges of his mouth. He glanced away for a second as if to collect his thoughts and continued, 'Now, take no notice of me blabbering on about my family. I'm sure you're not here to listen to me rambling on.' Cornelius clasped his hands before him and bowed his head slightly, 'How can I be of help?'

Rosie was keen to find out more about Hayden. 'So, is Hayden here today then?'

'No, he's returned to England.' Cornelius clamped his mouth shut and waited.

The antique timepieces on the walls ticked, and a large grandfather clock chimed out the hour. Cornelius looked pointedly at the clock. Rosie took the hint, 'Well, Cornelius, do you remember kindly agreeing to explain spreadsheets to me? Well, I was wondering if it was no trouble and if you aren't too busy––'

'Of course! My pleasure.' Cornelius greeted this change of subject with enthusiasm. He stepped over to the office chair by the desktop computer, dusted it off and chivalrously indicated for her to take a seat.

Rosie blinked behind her glasses as Cornelius pulled up screens on his computer to prove the magic of spreadsheets. His hands moved deftly across the keyboard. Rosie kept her eyes fixed on the screen. However, her mind was turning over all that she had learned that afternoon; Sam Bazley, the builder, was talking to the police, possibly arrested, although she didn't know that for sure. Sage was also a person of interest to the police. Indeed, she had lured Gerry up to the hill fort.

She glanced at Cornelius, who was now enjoying himself talking to her about formulas. She tried to tune back into what he was saying. Rosie glanced between him and the monitor. The grid on the screen reflected on his glasses, his face animated. But it made no sense. Rosie let his words wash over her as her mind drifted back to Hayden and his passionate interest in Celtic antiquities. Was Hayden aware of some ancient artefact up on the hill fort? Cornelius had been spotted with his metal detector up there. Did he know something? Was he helping Hayden? And now Hayden had suddenly gone back to England. Was that significant?

Rosie sighed deeply.

'Oh, I'm sorry, Rosie, I think I've lost you!' Cornelius smiled. 'I get a bit carried away with the old IT here. It's not just antiquities I'm interested in, you know. These machines are the future.' He affectionately patted his desktop computer and continued: 'Have you heard about a new worldwide information system – the Information Superhighway – they are developing in the States?'

Rosie looked back at him doubtfully. '*The Information Superhighway*? Sure, that sounds very *American* to me. I don't think that'll take off over here,' she sniffed dubiously. 'Anyway, I need to get back to that wee dog of mine. Thanks very much, Cornelius. You're a whizz on that thing.' Rosie nodded at the computer.

'My pleasure, Rosie. Just pop back if you need any help.'

Rosie was just about to respond when she looked out of the shop window and saw Sam Bazley skip quickly down the steps of the police station, looking up and down the street.

'I'll get off now; thanks again,' Rosie said, rushing out the door, eager to find out more about the builder who was the latest subject of police interest.

CHAPTER TWENTY-FIVE

Blaney's Blarney

That same afternoon, Mary Jo had decided to pick up some stationery supplies on her way home from school. The early spring sunshine faded, and the sky was transformed into a steely grey sheet as a chill wind blew along Rainbow Row. The nun was relieved to step into the bookshop and café. A welcome warmth, a hum of conversation, and the aroma of freshly baked goods met her at the shop's door.

'I'll be with you in a jiffy.' Marie called over from the counter by the kitchen area of the café adjoining the bookshop and stationers.

'No rush, I need a minute to find my list anyway.' Mary Jo called back as she fished in her bag for her shopping list. Once she had found it, she appeared absorbed in the note's contents in her hand. Her eyes moved between her list and the items on the shelves before her. However, her attention was really on the conversations around her. Her ears were straining to tune into what was being said between the ladies who sat in little huddles around the tables in the café. Mary Jo looked up from her list and scanned the café and shop. Mrs Blaney caught her eye. She raised the teacup in her hand by way of greeting, 'Sister.' She smiled sweetly and then switched her attention back to her companion. Both ladies sat at the table with their woollen coats buttoned up to the neck, pillbox-style hats on their heads and large handbags on their laps. They were speaking in hushed whispers. Mrs Blaney leaned in across the small table to talk with her confidante.

Mary Jo knew that Mrs Blaney and her friend Mrs Kirkpatrick, the Post Office Mistress, were sources of local news and gossip. Mary Jo edged closer. She didn't want to appear too interested in Mrs Blaney's chat, but she was keen to pick up any information concerning the murder. She wasn't disappointed.

'...terrible business.' Mrs Kirkpatrick from the post office paused to take a sip of tea.

'Yes, I heard it was carrying on for several months.' Mrs Blaney had just uttered the latest titbit and stopped momentarily to allow the full dramatic impact of what she was saying to settle on her companion.

'Never!' Mrs Kirkpatrick sat open-mouthed. Mrs Blaney inclined her head by way of acknowledgement, gratified that her snippet of gossip had the desired impact.

Mary Jo wondered who they were talking about. She picked up a jotter and flicked through it, pretending to eye up the number of pages and feel the quality of the paper. She made sure her eyes only moved between her note and the jotter. She maintained a neutral expression, not registering the slightest hint that she had overheard the latest snippet.

Mrs Blaney glanced at the nun, lowered her voice a fraction more, and said, 'Oh yes, I've been speaking to Katie, who works at the hotel now in Kilsheelan. Do you remember Katie, who used to work for me at the B&B? Well, she's working at that fancy hotel now.'

Mrs Kirkpatrick nodded earnestly, willing Mrs Blaney to get on with the main topic.

Well, she saw them together in the hotel over there. Quite a few times, apparently.'

Mrs Kirkpatrick gasped. 'Who would believe it? Some women have no shame, leading a good man astray like that.' Mrs Kirkpatrick tutted and seemed genuinely shocked. She sat with her hands in her lap, shaking her head.

'Well, I must get off now,' Mrs Blaney said, satisfied with the impact of her news. She gripped her purse, her knuckles showing white. 'I'm paying,' she announced.

'You are not. Indeed,' Mrs Kirkpatrick got up quickly, eyeballing her companion, and pulled out her purse like a cowboy in a dual.

Mary Jo saw the two women, amused by the familiar head-to-head in the race to pay first.

'*Put that away.*' Mrs Blaney spat out the words as she glared at Mrs Kirkpatrick's purse. She marched up to the counter with her tea companion hot on her heels. 'Take no heed of her,' Mrs Blaney nodded to the other woman.

Marie looked from one lady to the other, both standing proffering their purses.

'Take that.' Mrs Blaney pushed a note in Marie's palm and swiped her friend away with her free hand. Mrs Kirkpatrick stepped back to avoid a direct hit in the face, and in this split second of hesitation, Mrs Blaney had won. Her note was accepted, and the till made a satisfying chi-ching as payment was taken.

Both women left side by side, continuing to bicker in good humour about whose turn it was to pay. The bell above the door tinkled as the door banged shut.

Marie made it a personal rule not to comment on customers' conversations. She, too, had overheard the snatch of gossip, but she hummed quietly to herself as she wiped down the countertop. A few more customers came up to the counter to pay. Marie took their payment, and they left. Quiet then descended.

Mary Jo continued to browse the shelves and made a mental note to chat with Rosie about what she had heard and what it might mean. Who was carrying on with who? What did it all mean? Were the tittle-tattlers referring to Sage and the priest? Or Fiona and Gerry? Or Sam Bazley and Sage? Perhaps Mrs Bazley and Gerry? Or...who? It made the nun's head hurt. Mary Jo sighed deeply.

'Alright there, Sister?' Deirdre had appeared out of the kitchen. 'Did you hear what that oul biddy was saying? Never a good word to say about anyone.' Deirdre tutted and stacked some clean cups by the counter. She clearly did not share Marie's thoughts concerning gossip in the café.

Mary Jo greeted Deirdre with a smile.

'Who knows, Deirdre? I really wouldn't know myself. What do you think?'

The young woman paused momentarily – a clean tea towel draped over her shoulder.

'Well, I don't know who she is talking about, but I've gone to the police myself to tell them what I saw.'

Mary Jo turned away from the shelves of books and gave Deirdre her full attention.

'What was that then Deirdre?'

The young woman glanced around the shop and café, seeing that she, Marie and Mary Jo were the only occupants. She took a deep breath and began to speak.

'Well, I wouldn't tell just anyone, but as it's you, Sister, I'll tell you what I saw.'

Just then, the bell jingled, and Fiona Fitzgerald swept into the shop, a gust of chilly air blowing in after her.

'Hello, darlings!' she called to Marie and Deirdre, who stood open-mouthed. The usually amiable Mary Jo gritted her teeth and could only manage a tight smile. Fiona wore a long cream-coloured coat, pulling it around her dramatically, seeming to throw herself down onto a chair.

'I'm freezing! And absolutely parched! Any chance of a green tea, girls?' Fiona threw her head back and looked imploringly at her hosts. Marie was the first to respond.

'One green tea coming up!' Marie bustled into the kitchen.

Fiona spotted Mary Jo. 'Oh, hello, Sister! I didn't see you there, but that brown coat of yours does fade into the background somewhat. Such a shame you must wear such dull colours!'

Mary Jo was in no mood to discuss her sartorial options and instead just smiled.

'I'll take those. Thanks, Deirdre.' Mary Jo paid for her shopping. Mary Jo could see Fiona on the edge of her vision. The MEP was filing her nails as she waited for her green tea. Fiona paused to examine her long red fingernails. 'Such a shame about Gerry. I've just returned from Brussels and heard the news on the local radio.'

'Didn't you know already?' Deirdre asked.

Fiona smiled indulgently at the young woman. 'No, dear, I'm afraid small-town news from a backwater like Erin's Glen doesn't reach Brussels.'

Mary Jo bit her lip. She decided to leave the shop sooner rather than later. The story of what Deirdre saw would have to wait until another time.

Chapter Twenty-Six

Cause of Death

The next day was a Saturday, and Mary Jo was out, striding quickly through the town, past Rainbow Row, along the little old bridge over the flowing Abanculeen and on up the hill to Rosie's bungalow. The two friends had arranged to have breakfast together and discuss recent events. Mary Jo was under no illusion. Rosie was the detective – she was the sidekick. But the religious sister liked to think her contributions helped the truth to come out. What Mary Jo heard or saw on her frequent runs and walks were of invaluable help to Rosie. The amateur sleuth used all these fragments to help untangle the threads of impressions, ideas, memories, and feelings that formed in her own mind. These often added a missing spark to official investigations. A spark that usually ignited an illuminating light on the truth.

Mary Jo turned over recent events in her mind. The death of Gerry Macauley had unsettled many of the girls at the school where she worked. She had seen them huddled together during the breaks, telling each other stories about the *Shee*. Many were from families who blamed most of life's misfortunes on the little people. A sick cow, a failed crop, unseasonably harsh weather, lost objects or people. The cries and wails of the Banshee heralded family deaths. Mary Jo had grown up with the same stories and superstitions. Although officially and publicly, she scolded the girls for their silliness, privately, she kept an open mind. Her prayers for protection for the community she lived and worked in were more earnest in recent days.

Mary Jo's journey on foot to Rosie's home passed quickly, absorbed as she was in these thoughts. The door sprung open as she opened the gate into the small garden that fronted her friend's bungalow.

'Have you seen this?' Still in her dressing gown, Rosie was on the doorstep brandishing a local newspaper, *The Glen Herald*.

Mary Jo had not yet seen the paper and was keen to know the latest news – something significant, judging by Rosie's excitement.

Mary Jo followed her friend along the hallway into the large kitchen. Ziggy was already up out of his basket, tail wagging ferociously. Despite her eagerness to learn about the latest happenings, Mary Jo bent down to greet Ziggy as Rosie read the headlines.

Councillor Died of Natural Causes.

Rosie looked up, her eyes appearing owlish behind her reading glasses. Her grey hair, usually tamed neatly into a chin-length bob, circled her head like a fuzzy grey halo. She blinked, waiting for Mary Jo to respond to the news.

Both women dropped down onto kitchen chairs by the large pine table. It was set for breakfast, and Mary Jo was momentarily distracted by the welcome sight of the large teapot encased in its knitted cover.

'Well, that makes no sense at all.' Mary Jo was finally able to verbalise a response.

'Absolutely ridiculous,' Rosie agreed.

Satisfied by their mutual disgust at the headline's conclusion, Rosie checked the potato farls toasting under the grill, butter sizzling on their mottled floury surface. She turned some eggs in the pan and pushed some bacon next to them. Ziggy was much more interested in what was happening on the range and now ignored Mary Jo. The nun sat with the paper in front of her. A gritty image of Gerry Macauley looked back at her from the front page. She read out the article below the headline:

'Last night, Sergeant Kennedy of Erin's Glen police station released a statement. He has received information from the pathologist who, on a first examination, has concluded that Mr Macauley died from a heart attack. Sergeant Kennedy stressed that further in-depth examinations will need to take place. Due to the way Mr Macauley's body was laid out, the police will investigate further, but for now, the conclusion is that Mr Macauley's death was due to natural causes.'

Mary Jo tossed the paper across the table in contempt. She sat back in her chair, arms folded, recalling the vision of the dead councillor's body.

'Well, as you know, I found the poor man, and there was nothing natural about how he was laid out up on that hill fort. Somebody was involved––'

'Or *something*.' Rosie looked at Mary Jo meaningfully over her glasses, spatula in hand. She stood by the hob, her face flushed from its heat.

'Oh, don't you start!' Mary Jo tutted and shook her head with pursed lips. 'I've had all of that nonsense up to here.' Mary Jo tapped the top of her head.

'Aye, well, it probably *is* a load of nonsense. But you must admit, all that care someone took to lay him out *is* very odd. It's like somebody was offering him up to the *Shee*––'

Mary Jo was about to interrupt angrily, but Rosie raised her spatula to command attention and quiet. Mary Jo acquiesced with a pursed mouth and raised an eyebrow, not happy with this turn in the discussion.

Rosie continued, 'Not to say I believe in it all, but my point is *somebody* does. *Somebody* believes in the tales enough to go to all that effort of laying out the body with the candle, salt and what-not. And sure, that's a crime, interfering with a dead person. Sure, it's not natural, finding a body and deciding to perform some ceremony––'

'We don't know that.' Mary Jo interrupted.

'But you must admit it looks that way. Now, who would do that?'

Rosie turned back to her cooking and remained silent as she dished out the eggs, bacon and potato farls. Mary Jo poured the tea and looked eagerly at the large plate of glistening food coming her way. Ziggy began to whimper and looked meaningfully at his empty dish.

'Hold your whist!' Rosie scolded him gently, using a local expression. He sat silently now, eyes fixed on the full plates rapidly clearing as the ladies munched. Both thought through the implications of the latest news.

Rosie was chewing quickly, keen to update Mary Jo on what she had discovered the previous evening. When she swallowed the last mouthful of bacon and eggs, she focused on Mary Jo.

'I saw Sam Bazley, you know, the builder, come out of the station last night. I spoke to him briefly. He couldn't look me straight in the face, you know.'

Mary Jo, in turn, updated Rosie on what she had heard in the café the previous day.

'Aye, well, I'm not surprised. I don't like to carry gossip, as you know, especially from Mrs Blaney, but I overheard her talking about someone carrying on with someone else.' Mary Jo shook her head in puzzlement. 'Of course, it might not be connected. I suppose it could be anyone. The Lord himself only knows.'

Rosie considered the possibility that it could be Father Asher and Sage but dismissed the idea immediately. They wouldn't meet so publicly.

Rosie was thoughtful, 'Who would feel so angry, hurt, or determined to do away with Gerry? Suppose Gerry and Fiona had a thing going on? It's possible. Or was Aisling, Gerry's wife, carrying on with someone else? But, she was at her brother's house in Rocksheelan, looking after her nephews and nieces, the morning he was found. She went there the previous evening and stayed overnight with them. She's in the clear, it would seem.' Rosie looked quizzically at her friend. They both sat in silence, considering the possibilities.

'Let's think this through...' Rosie recalled what they knew so far, 'Gerry was found by yourself at about 6.45am. The pathologist reckons he died late the previous evening and that his body was moved up to the fairy ring and laid out not long after he died, the cause being a heart attack...'

'But who would go to all the effort with the body?' Mary Jo sighed and shook her head.

A sharp bark distracted them. Ziggy was by his bowl. He looked desperate now, tapping his paw pleadingly in the empty dish.

'Alright, we get the message!' Rosie stood up to sweep off the leftovers into his bowl, her mind only fractionally on her actions.

'Do you fancy a walk?' Rosie straightened up. Inspiration brightened her face.

'I've got an idea!'

Chapter Twenty-Seven

Covert Surveillance

A short while later in town, Mrs Blaney sat with Mrs Kirkpatrick in the chintzy dining room of her B&B. They were also rehashing events from the past twenty-four hours. As it was a Saturday, Mrs Kirkpatrick had the day off from her duties as postmistress. Her occupation provided her with endless titbits of gossip and inside knowledge that she relished sharing with her long-time friend, Mrs Blaney. Mrs Blaney had no guests and could speak openly with her confidante.

They sat opposite each other at a small round table covered in floral lacey cloths. Positioned in a little nook created by the bay window, they peered out onto the main street. The day promised rain. Heavy clouds scudded across a blue sky, creating a luminescent grey light that filtered through the gauzy curtains at the window. The light shining through the curtains created a dappled pattern on the women's faces as they held teacups aloft, both looking, not at each other but sideways out of the window.

'Terrible business with what happened to Gerry and with all these hippies in town, it's all very concerning....' Mrs Kirpatrick tutted. 'I don't like that tall, snooty one with the big dog. Never says a word. Wouldn't give you the time of day, that one.'

Mrs Blaney nodded, 'I don't trust her. She's floating around the town like one of the *Shee* herself. Sure, what's she like? She doesn't behave like a decent, normal woman at all. I think she's one of those cult leaders you hear about.'

Mrs Kirkpatrick was warming to this line of conversation. Her eyes widened, 'God only knows what they're up to in the fairy ring. It's not right. I'm sure she's behind all that business with poor Mr Macauley. I heard he was laid out weirdly. I reckon it was either the *Shee* themselves or that cult that did it. And I hold that woman responsible.' The postmistress was confident Sage was behind it all.

Both ladies paused and took a synchronized sip of tea from china cups adorned with violets.

'I see that Rosie is out on the loose again,' Mrs Kirpatrick commented, adjusting her position as she turned to watch Rosie's journey along the town's main street.

'Oh aye, and she's got the nun in tow. Why a woman of the church would go about with that nosey sinner, I will never understand.' Mrs Blaney shook her head and closed her eyes, adding dramatic emphasis to her lack of comprehension about this unlikely duo as she saw it.

'Sure, all they do is gossip. T'is a wonder the bishop doesn't sort that nun out. He should ban her from going about with that Rosie.' The postmistress tutted indignantly.

'Rosie O'Reilly is a bad influence on Mary Jo. She always was. Sure, I remember Rosie from school. Full of herself she was – just because she had a good memory, the teachers loved her – teachers' pet. That's all she was.' Mrs Blaney had a sour expression as she recalled her school memories concerning Rosie.

'Yes, there she goes. I knew it! Straight into the guards, going in to tell them how to do their job, no doubt. The nerve of the woman.' Mrs Kirpatrick warmed to her friend's dislike of Rosie and was keen to stir it up.

Mrs Blaney got to her feet and peered through the curtains more closely.

'Oh aye, yes, she's going in.' The B&B owner confirmed her friend's observations. She stood by the window for a few minutes and eventually sat opposite her friend, whose gaze remained fixed on the goings-on out in the street.

She drew her breath in sharply. 'Well, the bare-faced cheek of it!'

Mrs Blaney jumped up again to peer out of the window. 'What?' She quickly turned to look up and down the street, not wanting to miss out. 'What did you see?' she asked, almost pleading with her observant companion.

'Sure, it's that Sage out shopping like nothing's amiss. God, I wouldn't like her nerve in my back tooth. You should have seen her strolling up the street there with her shopping basket as if butter wouldn't melt in her mouth. And that poor man not cold in his grave yet.'

Both women made the sign of the cross rapidly as they recalled Gerry Macauley.

'She's away into that empty shop there.' Mrs Kirkpatrick kept a running commentary. 'Now, what is she doing in there? That woman doesn't know what to be at next.'

The two women shook their heads in disapproval.

Just as their commentary on the action out in the street lulled, the doorbell rang. Mrs Blaney bustled off to the door.

She re-entered the room, her face alight with pleasure.

'Ach, hello there, Mrs Stewart.' Mrs Kirpatrick was equally pleased to see another local information source.

'Well, ladies, I thought I'd pop round as soon as I was finished for the morning. The chemist shuts at midday, and I thought to myself, "I'll pop round to Mrs B and update her on the latest." Great to see you too, Mrs K. How are you doing?'

After a few pleasantries, tea pouring and cake offerings, Mrs Stewart got down to business.

'Well, you know that Rosie woman?' Intense nods from her companions who confirmed their familiarity with the parish secretary. 'Well, she was in my chemist's shop this morning.' The sales assistant paused, enjoying her friends' rapt attention.

'She was in giving me the third degree. You know what she's like. She's round asking more questions than the police themselves.' Mrs Stewart shook her head and turned her mouth down disapprovingly.

'What was she asking about then? Was she asking about Sam? He is in the spotlight at the moment.' Mrs Blaney asked.

'No, no, she wasn't asking about Sam. She was asking about Gerry. Of course, I am not supposed to divulge information about customers' prescriptions. Still, she does have a way of looking at you and asking things. Before you know it, you've given away things you never intended to say.' Mrs Stewart looked from one to the other of her companions, holding her hand belatedly over her mouth. Her big blue eyes were even bigger as she expressed her inability to resist Rosie's interrogation tactics.

'Ah, right.' Mrs Blaney assessed her friend, wondering how useful this would be. 'So, what was she asking about?'

'Well, she was asking about Gerry's regular prescription. He only had one for allergies. He was in good health, as it happens. I was amazed when I heard he had a heart attack. That's what's on the news now. So, it might not even be a murder case. Although I heard--'

Mrs B pre-empted her companion's news, 'Yes, yes—we know about the body. But what else did Rosie ask about?' News had come out about how Gerry was found.

The chemist shop assistant blinked and sniffed, disappointed that this snippet was not news. She added huffily, 'Well, that was it but I don't know why Rosie is bothering to nose around about his prescription. I probably shouldn't have told her anything.'

'Nosey Rosie. She can't help herself.' Mrs Kirkpatrick remarked uncharitably.

'Aye, you're right there.' Mrs Blaney nodded. She turned her attention back to Mrs Stewart, 'Well, I wouldn't worry. Sure, you haven't told her much, really, have you? '

'Not really. Mr Kinney doesn't like us talking to customers about other customers. But he wasn't there this morning.'

'And the customer in question *is* dead.' Mrs Kirkpatrick chimed in.

'Right so.' The other two chorused in unison, and the three ladies drank their tea and gazed out of the window, satisfied that the chemist shop assistant had done no wrong.

Chapter Twenty-Eight

Information, Communication and Technology

That same afternoon, Cornelius enjoyed a few quiet hours in his shop. This was how he liked it – peaceful. He sat behind his large mahogany desk in his office. He had a clear view of the sales counter and was alerted to a customer entering when the bell above the entranceway jingled. He sat back in the large leather office chair, relaxed and thoughtful. He considered the events of the past couple of weeks.

Unfortunately, recent occurrences had brought much more attention to the hill fort. He had enjoyed going up there before on quiet early mornings with his metal detector. There must be all sorts of treasure up there, secreted in that mound. It was fascinating. What a blasphemy to have diggers up there, rampaging across the land, churning up that ancient earth, crushing to dust the precious artefacts that had lain undisturbed for millennia.

Cornelius sat, letting the sound of ticking clocks and the creaks and groans of the old building soothe him. Some noises from the street drifted in. He was aware of an occasional car rumbling along the road, away from the town. His shop was further along from the central activity hub, and that's how he preferred it. That's how he always liked it, even as a child.

His mind drifted back to earlier in the week. He had decided it was better to keep Rosie close. She asked a lot of questions, and he was keen to know what answers she was getting. She was easy company anyway. He considered this for a moment and felt a stab of regret. Yes, he enjoyed Rosie's companionship. Of course, they were vastly different, and she was a bit of a chatterbox, but her ready humour, a keen eye for detail and ability to assess human nature accurately intrigued and entertained him. Even more reason to tread carefully, he cautioned himself. Don't get too attached, he reminded himself.

One thing that surprised him was her sudden interest in Cosmos. Cornelius had forgotten that Rosie even knew Cosmos, as he was a little older than her. Rosie would have gone to the girls' convent school, and Cosmos attended the boys' grammar class run by the Christian Brothers, so she must have remembered him from primary school.

Rosie seemed attracted by his technological expertise. He considered how all his family seemed to have a talent for picking up on the latest gadgets. His nephew, too. Hayden was a whizz with technology – a bright lad. Chip off the old block. Cornelius chuckled to himself. And people think I'm just an old-fashioned, eccentric gentleman. Corneilus chuckled again. Just then, the phone rang. He jolted in surprise. Despite the antiquity of the items in his shop, Cornelius had state-of-the-art technological equipment in his office, including a new style of phone that had a caller display. He glanced at it before he picked up the receiver and saw that it was his brother Cosmos.

'Well, talk of the devil,' Cornelius seemed to purr into the receiver.

He sat thoughtfully as his brother updated him on his news in Oxford. His eyes darted around his office and out to the shop as he listened. Erin's Glen was quiet on Saturday afternoon, and he appreciated the chance to chat privately with Cosmos, his older sibling.

'No, no worries this end, Cosmos. It's all in hand. Tell me, has the agreement gone through yet? Is the Head of the Department happy with the plans?' A modulated voice kept up a steady stream of dialogue on the other end. Cornelius nodded and affirmed that all was well.

'Rosie! I think she's quite taken with me, actually.' Cornelius laughed lightly as he smoothed back a stray strand of grey hair.

He laughed again. 'Oh, don't worry Cossie. I'm a confirmed bachelor. You are the main actor in the romance dramas!'

There was the soft rumble of laughter from the other end, and after saying his adieus, Cornelius put the phone down softly.

He glanced around his desk and out to the shop. Assured that he was alone, he slowly put his fingers into a small pocket at the front of his ornate waistcoat. He pulled out a small key on a chain and unlocked one of the drawers at the side of his desk.

He peered into the shallow, tidy drawer. One object dominated the small, neat space.

A rarely used mobile phone.

CHAPTER TWENTY-NINE

No Kidding

Urged on by Rosie, the two friends – Rosie and Mary Jo, accompanied by Ziggy – trotted off to the fairy ring. Rosie knew she needed to trust her instincts, and her instincts were leading her to Toddy's cottage. She was worried about him.

They tried to speak to the police about Toddy, but the sergeant was dismissive. Rosie decided to take the situation into her own hands. Mary Jo agreed, and so, in response to Rosie's suggestion, they decided to go and find out what was going on with the misanthropic custodian of the fort.

As they entered the woods, no familiar curl of smoke came from Toddy's cottage. Usually, he would be outside its doors, mending a bike, skinning a rabbit, or gutting a fish, but not today. In fact, the forest seemed eerily quiet. There was no birdsong. The day was flat, cold and grey. Both the women felt uneasy and Ziggy also seemed wary. His customary bouncy trot was replaced by careful padding through the foliage, ears pricked and eyes wide.

'It's like the forest has its moods,' Rosie remarked as she glanced around, her eyes taking in all. The familiar details, 'It always feels slightly different each time I come here. Today, it feels quiet and watchful.'

Mary Jo nodded in agreement.

Both women made their way along the dirt path through a mulch of leaves towards the old cottage set in a clearing among the gnarled trees and overgrown weeds. As they got closer, it looked even more dilapidated and neglected than usual. The front door was ajar, probably pushed open by the recent wind. A hinge had come away, and the door hung at a crooked angle. The paint had peeled away, and the bare boards of the worn old door were exposed to the elements.

Rosie gingerly pushed the door open wider, and they peered inside. In the low, steely light of the cold morning, the interior was gloomy and dark. The trio stepped inside and moved indoors slowly. Ziggy suddenly began to bark and strained at the lead, desperate to run through the cottage.

'Shush, what's up with you?' Rosie pulled him back on the lead and looked hard at him. Ziggy swallowed with a gulp and sat down beside his mistress, keeping his topaz eyes fixed on her.

When quiet had descended again, Mary Jo whispered. 'Do you hear that?

Rosie's eyes were roving around the unkempt room. 'What?' she whispered back.

Mary Jo waited a moment with her finger to her lips. Ziggy made some little strangled sounds in the back of his throat as if he was trying to stifle his barks. He stood, unnerved, glancing around, the whites of his eyes showing.

Rosie couldn't hear anything. She was shocked at the state of the place and felt desperate to sneeze. Her nose twitched as she contained herself, straining her ears to detect what Mary Jo had heard.

'That.' Mary Jo whispered.

Rosie was just about to remonstrate and point out that she could hear nothing when she detected a slight sound that seemed to come from the bedroom. Both women looked at each other in alarm, unsure what creature could be making such a pitiful, weak cry. Ziggy took charge. He marched off, pulling Rosie after him in the direction of the sound with Mary Jo behind them.

It was more distinct now, shaky but louder. A slight mewing sound that came from the back room. As they entered the room, a tiny baby goat with slender legs appeared from under the bed, bleating and mewing, crying piteously.

'Oh, the poor wee thing.' Mary Jo went off to get the little kid a saucer of water. Ziggy barked again and was hushed by his owner. The kid scuttled past them and out the door. Mary Jo, who stood with a small dish of water, watched as the leggy creature scampered out to freedom.

'Nice thought, but he's off to find his mother.' Rosie remarked, nodding at the dish of water. Ziggy looked after the kid, shaking his head in bewilderment.

'Well, it's not every day that happens. Judging by the hoof prints around here, he's been in here a while.' Mary Jo looked down at her feet, careful about where she was treading. Nature had taken its course, and the goat had left behind more than footprints.

'Well, it's to be expected in the countryside,' Rosie said placidly as they walked back through to the living room and kitchen.

Mary Jo looked around carefully, 'Well, Toddy's not here anyway.'

'Thanks, Sherlock,' Rosie remarked dryly. Mary Jo just tutted and rolled her eyes.

'Look at the state of that.' The fireplace had attracted Mary Jo's attention now. She walked closer to the grate to investigate. 'It looks like a jackdaw's nest was up in the chimney, and it's fallen into the grate. I hope there was no fire lit at the time. It must have come down in all that wind the other night.'

Rosie stood gazing at it and shaking her head at the mess it had created. She walked over to where Mary Jo was crouched down and spotted some postcards smudged with soot and dust. Rosie blew off the powdery debris and examined the picture on the front; it was a green and grey inky sketch of some fairy-looking creature with the title *Earth Fairy* written below it. Rosie had seen these around the town. All this New Age stuff was getting immensely popular. She sniffed and turned one over. A scrawl of large, loopy handwriting covered the back of the card. There were a handful of the cards, all with handwritten verses on the back.

'These could be significant,' Rosie peered closely at the handwritten notes. Mary Jo looked up from examining the nest in the grate.

Rosie's eyes moved rapidly across the card in her hand as she deciphered the script. Mild interest quickly transformed into rapt attention, followed by alarm. Rosie looked up at Mary Jo, eyes wide.

'Oh my God, Toddy, what have you got yourself into?'

Mary Jo took the notes from her friend, keeping her eyes fixed on Rosie for a second. Rosie appeared transfixed to the spot. Mary Jo looked down at the notes, her brow puckering as she concentrated on reading them. Her questioning expression quickly transformed into one of shock,

'Right, well, back to the police station, then.' Mary Jo was already out the door, leaving Rosie and Ziggy in her wake.

Chapter Thirty

Echoes from the Past

The next day was Sunday, and Rosie decided to have a quiet day at home after attending Mass and taking Ziggy out for his walk. 'No amateur sleuthing today, wee man,' she had warned Ziggy after their uneventful morning constitutional. The numbers at Mass had gone down again, and Father Asher appeared subdued. The sermon today was short and much more conventional than usual.

Rosie's visit to the police station the previous day had not been entirely satisfactory. Dan had greeted her grumpily. 'Right, more paper to check,' he had remarked ungratefully. He took the notes off her sullenly, stuffing them into an evidence bag. Although the reception of her detective offering was received ungraciously, the visit to the police station was worth it for the information she managed to wrangle out of Dan. During their conversation, Dan let slip that Gerry had been found with an empty medication bottle in his pocket along with the note from Sage, inviting him to the fairy ring to discuss the proposed development. Rosie had not told Dan she was aware of the note already, but the empty bottle was a valuable snippet of information. After being grudgingly given these titbits, Rosie had lost no time checking out the details of Gerry's prescription with Mrs Stewart at the chemist. It was much easier to get information out of her. Rosie felt a stab of resentment that the police did not share what they knew more willingly and openly with her.

Rosie remembered this as she dusted the photos and knickknacks on the shelves of her display cabinet in her living room. She sighed angrily, her recollection of the previous day stirring up her wrath. Ziggy sat bolt upright on the sofa, sensitive to his owner's uncharacteristically sullen mood.

'The cheek of the man!' she remarked to her canine companion. Rosie began to bang down her ornaments with more force than necessary, recalling the previous day: 'Telling me off for going into Toddy's cottage. Me out doing the work the police should be doing themselves and then having a go at me.' Ziggy just shook his head ruefully and gazed outside.

With all the bric-a-brac in the display cabinet now sparkling, Rosie stepped back with her hands on her hips to admire her work. After her monologue, an eerie silence descended. Rosie had not shaken off the suspicion that someone was watching her home, which unsettled her. In times like this, when the bungalow was quiet, Rosie felt uneasy, so she decided they needed some music to change the atmosphere and lighten her mood. She looked at her watch, 'Ah great, the Golden Oldies Show starts at 3 pm.' Rosie shook her duster, and Ziggy sneezed as she bustled out of the kitchen to switch on the radio.

Rosie hummed and sang along with the old hits from a few decades before. She sang along with Doris Day at top volume, the gusty tempo of the song transferring her indigent mood into happy nostalgia. 'My mother loved this one,' she told Ziggy, who had now retreated to his basket with his nose between his paws. He raised one eyebrow to acknowledge her.

'Ah, they don't make them like that anymore.' Rosie was now cleaning down the kitchen countertops, enjoying the music and memories it brought back.

'We're going to slow it down now, just a little bit, with a favourite for all you romantics out there: The Puffins sing their all-time classic, "Earth Fairy." Enjoy, folks!.' As the melody began, Rosie stopped her vigorous cleaning and stood still, listening to the lyrics.

Earth Fairy, Earth FairyMy darling love, meet me by the tree.I'm just a fool, a fool in love with you.

The slow rhythm and sentimental lyrics tugged at Rosie's heartstrings and stirred up some memories of dances in the old village hall, long gone now. She hummed along with the melody; her brow creased as she brought old, long-gone dalliances and romances to mind.

'Foolish nonsense,' she chided herself for her sentimentality. The song's title also brought back a more recent memory of the image on the postcards from the previous day. Rosie began to make some connections. She wasn't yet sure how all the dots connected, but she saw some significant lines join up. Rosie had a box of old photos. So, rather than rush off to the next household chore, she would get those out. Recent events had made her go back in time and re-examine some memories. She turned them over in her mind, considering each recollection carefully. Rosie considered how so much of what happens in the present has its seeds in the past, especially in a small community like Erin's Glen.

Rosie stood stock still in the middle of her neat kitchen, listening to the end of the ballad. The slow crooning drone of the singer and backing band fired up the images from the past. Rosie recalled the etiquette of 'courting.' The dances, picnics in summer, walks out into the countryside, perhaps a sherry in the lounge of The Thatch bar when you turned twenty-one. For Rosie, the years between her sixteenth birthday and the day she got the key to the door on her twenty-first were a happy, carefree and giddy time. As she entered her twenties, the realities of life kicked in. Friends got married and were busy with the demands of babies and husbands. Others left Erin's Glen. Most of her friends and acquaintances left the town. Work was hard to find, and it was to be expected that young people would go off in search of a better life across the water in England or further away in America or Canada. Rosie's sister went, meaning Rosie stayed behind to look after their mother. Rosie had no heart to leave her alone in Erin's Glen.

Rosie shook off her mood, which was turning from nostalgic to maudlin, and went off searching for the box of photos that could be a key to what had been going on recently in Erin's Glen. Despite the lack of support or encouragement from the local police, Rosie was not deterred. She was determined to find out the truth of what was going on. So, despite it being a day of rest, Rosie followed her sleuthing instincts and got the ladder out for the loft.

'Right here we go.' She called to Ziggy as he stood at the base of the ladder, looking up at his mistress as she climbed up into the roof space. He sat patiently as boxes got pushed about on the dusty floor.

'Ah, this is the one.' Rosie appeared triumphantly at the hatch with a tin full of photos tucked under her arm. She descended the ladder carefully. After hurriedly popping it back into the attic, she plopped herself down on the sofa and quickly pulled out old photos. Images of fresh-faced friends beaming out at her took her back in time. Despite them all being in black and white, Rosie recalled the scenes in full colour. The photos were a catalyst for her internal photographic memory. Her sister was the photographer and seemed to be snapping pictures constantly for a couple of years, much to Rosie's annoyance at the time. Still, she was grateful now, for these visual triggers evoked powerful memories from her youth. She laughed at the big spotted skirts she liked to wear and the little hats she could balance on her head. She gasped at the height of her heels and recalled how ridiculous it was to try to walk in the countryside on these towering stilettos. All the photos were of groups and couples. People with arms draped around each other, smiling and laughing. She could hear their voices in her memory, the endless banter and jokes. The same jokes over and over that no one got tired of.

Rosie smiled as she looked at photos of her old mother standing outside in the garden with a younger Rosie while her sister took the picture. A few images were blurred or taken at odd angles, and Rosie recalled her lack of technical prowess even then. 'I'll have taken those. Sure, I was useless with anything mechanical back then, too,' she remarked aloud, chuckling at herself.

Just as she was laughing at her ineptitude with technology, she found what she was looking for: a photo of a couple who had gone their separate ways in adulthood. But perhaps they hadn't. Maybe they were still in touch now. Perhaps their relationship was influencing the present more than people might ever suspect.

Chapter Thirty-One

In the Clear

The previous day, Dan eventually got to the bottom of the two boxes of paperwork his boss had left him to go through. The pile of papers that could be significant was blessedly small. Paperwork was not Dan's strong point, and he struggled to remain in a reasonable mood as the afternoon wore on. To top it off, Rosie O'Reilly, the nun, and even the blasted dog were here telling him how to do his job. 'Like I'm some sort of green-behind-the-ears-rookie.' He bristled with anger. 'The cheek of them, noseying around in Toddy's house, and the man not even there.' Such were the thoughts Dan had as he reflected on his work week.

Dan, too, had decided to make the most of his rest day. He had taken himself off for a few hours of peace, sitting with his rod by the river far away from the town. A spot of fishing would help him think straight.

He sat alone on a fold-out canvas stool with the rod in his hand, turning over recent events. He took a deep breath. There was a chill in the air, but he was grateful to feel a fresh breeze on his face after being cooped up in the office all day yesterday. Being out in the open helped him think. He couldn't get his head into gear, sitting at a desk with a typewriter in front of him and a pile of paper looking back at him. He had space out here to mull things over, and that's precisely what he was doing today.

He had been sorting box number one when Rosie turned up all of a bother about some notes she had found in Toddy's place. He had warned her about going uninvited into peoples' unoccupied homes but had thanked her civilly and put the notes in an evidence bag. He gave them a quick look and saw that they were some poems. *Poems!* For goodness' sake, he needed hard evidence, not someone's namby-pamby efforts at being a poet. He had taken them off her and put them away safely. What else did she want? It bothered him to think back to how she had slammed out the door without a goodbye or anything. The nun had just waved at him and smiled. But she would. She was trained to smile at everybody. Sure, they were told not to be so scary these days. It's not like when he was a kid...but that was another story.

He pulled his thoughts back to the contents of the box. He rushed back to it as soon as he got rid of Rosie. Sam Beazley could be accused of being disorganised, lackadaisical or even downright lazy regarding paperwork and accounts, but that was about it. Dan had found plans for the tourist centre, but there were no surprises there. The retreat centre for Sage was another thing, but not a crime. Of course, the figures involved would need to be gone into more thoroughly, and on *first* inspection, there was nothing amiss.

Dan's train of thought was disturbed now by some movement under a tree on the other side of the river. It was too big to be a bird or a squirrel, and there was no livestock out here. Dan stared over at the big oak tree, its branches reaching down almost to the ground, the first buds of spring just starting to unfurl. He couldn't see underneath it clearly as it was in complete shadow from the heavy drooping branches. After a few moments of staring over at the tree, his eyes got tired, and Dan brought his mind back to events from the previous day.

The only thing that surprised him was the priest and Sage's plans for some new-fangled retreat centre near the hill fort. Now, *that* was news to him. Before his discovery in the box of paperwork, he had not heard of any plans for a retreat centre, especially not one run by the priest and that hippie leader, Sage. They had kept that quiet. Now, what was all that about? He had questioned the priest and even got on to the bishop.

The priest wasn't going anywhere fast, as he had been told to stay in the parish, so Dan decided to question him again the next day. He would also get onto Sage again. Dan decided to visit Sage at her make-shift camp and see her in situ, having an informal nose about it. Those postcards Rosie had brought around yesterday were like something Sage would have up at her place, all that New Age stuff. Dan thought back to the contents of the written notes on the back of the cards. Now, that was interesting. Dan felt a vague bristling of his conscience. He had not thanked Rosie for her contributions and decided to ring her from the station and apologise. She was a good oul stick, really, and she meant well. He should have been more polite.

The tree across from the river caught his attention again. There was definite movement under that tree. He cursed himself for forgetting his binoculars. There is something else I need to check out tomorrow, he reminded himself. It was getting dark now, and his wife was expecting him home for the Sunday dinner.

'There might be another murder in Erin's Glen if I'm not back for my dinner!' he chuckled as he packed his fishing gear. The cooler box where he put anything he caught was empty, but he had found the time alone therapeutic, so it was well spent.

He looked at the big oak tree again. A soft glow came from underneath its heavy branches. 'Probably just kids', he told himself, packing up his bag.

He was just about to sling his bag over his shoulder and pick up his rod when he saw Mary Jo come plodding down the path along the river, a light set into a band around her head. He recognised her tall figure and her signature brown tracksuit.

She stopped in front of him, breathing heavily as she got her breath back.

'Have you heard the news, Dan?' The nun panted the words.

The off-duty policeman's face stared back blankly.

'Sam Beazley is on a life support machine in the hospital.'

Chapter Thirty-Two

That Monday Morning Feeling

Monday mornings were always busy at Erin's Glen Post Office. The spacious shop accommodated a postal counter and a tourist information point. Racks of postcards, brochures, and books with local information and maps filled the space. Light flooded in from the tall windows that reached up to the high ceiling. Stone arches graced the broad double doors, and the interior was bright, airy, welcoming. Mrs Kirkpatrick was behind the postal counter this morning, dealing out stamps, weighing parcels and completing forms with some haste. She wasn't in a welcoming mood and was keen to clear the queue that had formed before the post office opened.

Mrs Blaney wasn't in the queue. She browsed the racks of cards and inspected the small selection of pens, whiling away the time until her friend was free for a few moments and the post office was clear.

The last customer lingered by the counter, eager for a chat. Mrs Kirkpatrick was nodding rapidly, grinning ferociously, willing the elderly gentleman to clear off so she could catch up with Mrs Blaney.

'Right so, right so, well you get off home now, Mr Pearse. Don't be getting a chill now. Cheerio!'

At last, the poor old chap ran out of small talk and shuffled off, looking crestfallen. The heavy door had not yet shut behind him when Mrs Blaney rushed to the counter.

'Have you heard?' she raised her arched eyebrows enquiringly at her friend.

Mrs Kirpatrick tutted in response and nodded, confirming that she had been privy to the latest shock news in Erin's Glen.

'What do you make of it?'

Mrs Kirkpatrick was about to open her mouth to answer when the oak door to the post office creaked open. A tall, skinny boy of about seventeen walked into the post office. His face was thin and spotty, and he smirked as he approached the counter. Both women stared at him, and he slunk back in response to their intense looks.

'Come on now, son. What do you want?' Mrs Kirkpatrick called impatiently over the counter.

'Can I have a phhhh...'

Mrs Blaney moved closer and kept a relaxed pose with her arm up on the counter, watching the young man with mild amusement. Mrs Kirkpatrick stared at him, unsmiling, tapping her fingers.

He started again, 'Can I have a phhhh...'

'First class stamp?' Mrs Blaney offered.

He shook his head.

'A phone...' He began again.

Quick as a flash, Mrs Kirkpatrick produced a phone card. He stopped trying to enunciate the words and looked relieved. He peered into the palm of his hand and counted out his coins agonisingly slowly.

The two women shook their heads as he ambled off, his large trainer boots making his legs look stick thin and accentuating his bowlegs.

'Couldn't stop a pig in the road, that one.' Mrs Blaney giggled at her remark and then carried on, apparently in good humour despite the disturbing news spreading fast over the town. She directed her attention back to her friend and pronounced, 'Well, I reckon that hippie one up the road is behind it.'

Mrs Kirkpatrick considered this, blinking behind her thick glasses, which looked like the bottoms of glass bottles. She nodded, 'Terrible business. But I suppose it's the quiet ones you need to watch.'

Mrs Blaney raised her eyebrows again and shrugged, 'Well, that's us out of the frame then!'

'True enough, no one could describe us as quiet!'

And with Mrs Kirpatrick's quip, both women laughed so hard they had to get their hankies out to dry their eyes.

'Ah, I knew you'd give me a lift this morning. You know how to chase the Monday blues.' Mrs Blaney laughed as she rushed out the door. She wanted to ensure that the rest of Erin's Glen was kept up to date on her opinions regarding the latest developments in the town.

***

Over in the parish office, Rosie was grappling with her own low mood this Monday morning. The box file of accounts and papers Father Asher had left with her the previous week still sat there and needed to be tackled.

Cornelius had shown her how spreadsheets worked on his computer. She knew she would need to bite the bullet and switch on the parish office machine to look at these marvels that would help her get the accounts into some order. But not yet. She had more pressing matters on her mind.

Rosie sat gazing out of the window, thinking. Mary Jo had phoned her at home the previous evening to tell her about Sam. Rosie had slept poorly, turning over in her mind what it all meant. Who would want to do away with Gerry and now Sam? Someone who disapproved of the new tourist centre. The obvious people who came to mind were Sage and her group of eco-warriors. Would they really go to such lengths to oppose the centre's building?

The office was quiet today, and the house was silent. She had let herself in with her key and assumed Father Asher was out. She checked the diary. He had no engagements this morning, but she never knew with him. Unlike Father Gerard, the old priest who used to be at the parish, he didn't keep her informed about his movements. Rosie wished he was here to confide in. The previous day, she had fallen into a low mood thinking about the past. Going back through those old photos and then hearing the news about Sam capped it all off.

'There's no way I'm in the mood for spreadsheets this morning. Let's get to the bottom of what's happening.'

Then Rosie did what she usually did to help her think. She put the kettle on.

The presbytery kitchen was large and old-fashioned. The cupboards were painted a creamy white, the paint thick and lumpy from layers of gloss applied over the decades. An enormous range dominated one wall and provided a steady source of heat in the house that was still without central heating. The room had a familiar smell of bread baking, and Rosie breathed in the comforting aroma.

Feeling brighter with a big mug of tea in her hand, she got on with trying to piece together the fragmented memories trickling piecemeal into her mind, prompted by the photos she had looked at yesterday, the old melody on the radio, and the handwriting on the postcards she had found at Toddy's. These were the postcards she had handed to the police. Despite Dan's initial reluctance to acknowledge their importance, she *knew* the poems written on the cards were significant and she had committed each verse to memory.

She closed her eyes and re-read the words on each *Earth Fairy* card she had looked at a few days before. With her photographic memory, she could see them in her mind's eye as if they were in front of her. Rosie had her eyes shut tight, her brow furrowed in concentration as she recalled the content of each verse and the handwriting style. Each card contained a short poem, most of which were written in blue ink with an expansive, swirling script. She recalled the first one.

In shadows deep, where spirits roam,
A whispered lament, a spectral moan.
You, kin of blood and ancient kin,
Have let your ancestors down within.

Rosie knew that Toddy's family had lived in that cottage for generations. There was always talk about them being some sort of custodians of the fairy ring. Rosie hadn't taken much notice, dismissing such tales as a way for the family to find purpose for their presence in the woods. But it looked like Toddy took this role seriously. Would it be serious enough to murder someone? Did Toddy write these himself, perhaps? But Rosie reckoned Toddy's literacy skills were just about adequate for reading the notes, certainly *not* penning them. Someone with an extravagant and flowing style of handwriting wrote them. No, Toddy couldn't have written these himself. With her eyes closed, Rosie studied the style of handwriting in her memory. It was familiar, but from where? She gritted her teeth in frustration and brought to mind the following note:

The sacred bonds that once held firm,
Now strained by your neglectful wrong.
Regret, a phantom, lingers nearby,
As ancestral voices shed a tear.

These notes must have tortured poor Toddy if he felt that he had failed to protect the fairy ring from the developers, but the following note offered some hope:

Yet, in the shadows, there's a chance,
To mend the ties, the ethereal dance.
Seek redemption in the moonlit night,
Restore the bond and set things right.

Rosie's photographic memory was doing her proud now as she continued to sheaf through the notes in her mind's eye. The next one returned to the threatening tone of the first card:

Listen close to the ghostly plea,
A warning sent across a mystery.
Follow the path, heed the decree.
Or haunted, forever, you shall be.
Through the fields,
let your footsteps trace,
Banshees' Bloom holds a serene embrace.
In each petal, tales of serenity unfurl,
A respite found in nature's quiet swirl.

Rosie considered what this meant. She wasn't totally sure, but she thought Banshees' Bloom was a tall plant with delicate white flowers. She would go to the library later and find a book on local plants and check that out.

It was the next card with the longest poem that alarmed her most:

Gather moonlit blossoms,
soft and bright,
As Luna weaves her enchanting light.
Banshees' Bloom,
a remedy rare,
To bring sweet dreams to Gerry's lair.
In a cauldron of midnight's brew,
Infuse the petals,
let sorrows undo.
A potion potent,
with the moon's gentle zest,
To grant Gerry's weary soul sweet rest.

Rosie could picture Toddy alone in that cottage, haunted by spectres from the past. She felt for him, the poor, lonely man that he was. But Toddy was no poet.

So, *who* had written those poems?

Chapter Thirty-Three

Blues and Twos

Over at the police station, Dan was struggling with his own Monday morning blues. Any peace he had enjoyed out fishing had been destroyed by the news Mary Jo had brought to him by the river last night. Sam had been in a nasty car accident out near Rocksheelan. He had been coming back from a Gaelic football practice that he went to every Sunday afternoon. No other vehicles were involved. The police on the scene from the neighbouring town had concluded that Sam had lost control of the car. Further initial investigation revealed the brakes had been tampered with – foul play needed to be looked into.

Dan's first task today was to ring the hospital to find out how Sam was doing. Sam was now off life support and stable. The swelling on his brain had subsided, and his lungs were now functioning independently. He was a young, strong man, and Dan was hopeful he would fully recover. However, he needed to get to the bottom of what had happened. Of course, he also still needed to clarify the circumstances surrounding Gerry Macauley's death. If it was natural causes, who arranged his body in a ceremonial fashion?

It wasn't yet 10 am, and Dan was already feeling overwhelmed. The second box of paperwork from Sam's office would have to wait. If Sam's crash were connected with all this nasty business concerning Gerry, then Sam would be in the clear. It appeared someone wanted to do away with the builder, too. Now, why would that be?

The police officer's thoughts returned to the retreat centre plans. Would Sage want to get Gerry out of the way to build her own eco-retreat centre? He thought these hippie types were all about peace and love. Maybe not when it comes to business, he thought cynically.

He pushed away from the desk and decided to go for a wander. He needed to check out what was under that tree across from the river. He'd get on the bike, ride out towards the river path, ramble around in the field and check out what he had seen the previous day. Dan brightened at the thought of an hour or so out and about in the fresh air.

More out of a general sense of duty rather than following up on anything specific, Dan turned down past Rainbow Row to see what was happening this Monday morning. He reached the far end of the street and paused outside a shop that had lain empty for a few months. He spotted a battered white van outside the empty shop. There was a young man in overalls painting its frontage. He glanced up at Dan but said nothing. He returned his attention to his slow, methodical painting. The door was wide open, and Dan peered in. He saw that the shop was still empty. He stood watching the young man paint a silhouette of a figure on the front panel by the side of the door. He watched as the talented lad, obviously an artist, brought a wraithlike creature in green to life. Dan recognised the picture. After a few moments of watching the artist at work, he interrupted him.

'What is that?'

'I'm just following instructions. It's nothing illegal,' the artist smirked at Dan and continued painting.

'Whose shop is this?'

The young man pointed up at the outline of the shop's name, ready to be filled in with paint later. Dan could make out the words, 'Sage's Garden Pantry.'

'So, is it a greengrocer's shop then?' Dan asked.

The young man smirked again and shrugged, 'Aye, something like that. Herbs, oils, juices, health foods, that sort of thing. Are you after something in particular then?'

Dan shook his head quickly. Definitely not the sort of greengrocers he had in mind. The green wraith-like image that the artist was bringing to life transfixed him. How weird. But he reminded himself it was just an odd coincidence. None of it meant anything. He got back on his bike and cycled off up along the high street and out towards the river.

He made his way over the little humpbacked bridge that took him to the side of the river opposite to his fishing spot the previous day. He leaned his bike against the dry-stone wall closest to the field and waded through the long, damp grass. The giant oak tree was not giving away any of its secrets until he was well under its branches. There were a few signs of recent activity under here: some food wrappers, a small, scorched spot that might have accommodated a small fire and an area of flattened grass where a sleeping mat might have been. Whoever was under here had packed up and moved on. Dan ducked under the branches back out into the weak spring sunshine that was breaking up the grey cloud of the morning.

He looked across the field, his eyes following the course of the sparkling river, taking in the town's landmarks, and surveying its familiar skyline. He could pick out the roof of St Brigid's church, the familiar rows of shops and houses and some new roads that spiralled off up towards the hills and the mountain Slievecairn that dominated the north end of the town. To the side of the mountain was the silhouette of the hill fort with its signature tree at the top. The mound of the fort, highlighted by the lone tree, was usually a familiar and comforting sight. But not today. Dan gazed across at Erin's Glen and realised there was so little he understood what was happening there recently.

Chapter Thirty-Four

Stitch Up

Rosie was looking forward to the weekly craft group gathering more than usual this week. Her low mood on Monday was beginning to dissipate. She felt like she was getting close to solving the mystery of Gerry's death, but she wasn't there just yet. She had passed on what she was certain about to the police, but the slippery strands of half-known facts, memories and snippets of information gave her the most trouble. These were too intangible to talk to Dan or Seargeant Kennedy about just yet. These impressions lay just below her level of consciousness and were distracting her from her work and chores at home. She got so absorbed in her thoughts that she became even more absent-minded than usual. For the sake of her health and well-being, she'd be glad to get this case wrapped up, or goodness only knows what she might do.

Such were the thoughts that filled Rosie's mind as she packed up her craft bag, ready for her activities that evening. The crafters in the group usually worked together as a community to create items for the next big town celebration. The next date on Erin's Glen calendar was May Day. As usual, it had a floral theme that befitted the spring flavour of the seasonal event. Rosie had decided to make some felt flower brooches to sell during the May Day event. The celebrations would include food and drinks stalls, dancing, music and a procession up to the hilltop. This year, it would take on a new significance, of course. Rosie hoped that Gerry's memory could be honoured and that all the mystery surrounding his death would be solved before then.

'Now you stay here and guard the house.' Rosie instructed a resentful Ziggy as she checked around the kitchen to ensure she hadn't left anything on. She backed out the front door with her large craft bag clutched in front of her.

The night was clear and crisp, and the last traces of daylight were fading as Rosie drove down to Rainbow Row to join her friends. She was warmed by the sight of the shop all aglow, standing out from its shuttered neighbours closed for the night.

The bell tinkled as she entered, and she was greeted by Mary Jo, who sat serenely with empty hands in her lap. Marie bustled about with plates of cakes, and little Deirdre struggled under the weight of a massive pot of tea that was making its way to the table in the centre of the group.

'Hello there, Rosie!' she called over, 'Perfect timing as usual. I've just got the tea wet.' Deirdre plonked the pot down with a groan.

Marie sat down heavily, weary from her day in the shop. She was beginning to explain, 'Well, ladies, I hope you don't mind, but--'

Just then, the doorbell jingled again, and two familiar faces entered the room.

'Hello there, I was just going to tell the group you would join us tonight.' Marie smiled warmly, and Deirdre moved chairs around to make room for the two women who had just entered the room.

Rosie and Mary Jo, not often lost for words, watched as the two women, both new to the group, sat down, looking around with expectant faces.

One of the unexpected faces belonged to Aisling Macauley, Gerry's widow. She looked at Rosie and Mary Jo, noting their expressions. She correctly guessed what was running through their minds.

'I know you're probably surprised I'm here, in fact, that *we're* here,' she paused and smiled at her companion, Cathy Bazley. Cathy, round-faced with a thick mop of curly blonde hair, beamed around at the group. 'But the truth is even grieving widows or near-widows need to get out. I miss Gerry terribly, and the evenings are the worst.' Aisling paused again. She was a small, neatly dressed woman with a thin, drawn face. However, her brown eyes, framed by long lashes, were bright and hopeful. She blinked away tears, took a breath and continued. 'I was here the other day looking for new account books, and Marie suggested I join you. I've been working to keep my mind off what's happened recently. I thought I deserved a night off.'

'And sure, I've been the same these past few days.' Cathy Bazley chimed in now. 'I've been up at the hospital day and night. I'm like the Lady of Mercy, I am. Sam's doing alright, and the nurses up there chased me out, telling me I needed a break from being the Angel with the Lamp. Aisling here has been solid as a stone. Taking turns to sit with Sam. In fact, she suggested we come along here, so I thought, 'Why not?'

'Why not, indeed!' Mary Jo piped up, 'It's great to have you both here, and I'm sure it will do you good. And we need plenty of craft contributions to sell on the big day!'

'Exactly! That's what I thought, all elbows greasing the decks!' Cathy beamed round again, her shiny face aglow in the soft light from the lamps lining the shelves.

There was a break in the conversation while tea was poured and cakes served.

Aisling looked around at the assembled group. She was aware of some of the local gossip and wanted to clear the air. She shifted in her seat and cleared her throat. 'I'm sure you've heard a lot of rumours about me.' All those assembled shook their heads vigorously. They were too ashamed or embarrassed to admit they had.

Cathy, Sam's wife, cut in again, 'Ah, no need to be embarrassed; we decided to join forces to show the local gossip mongers – present company excluded, of course – that we are both faithful wives. We want to know the truth of what's happened to our husbands. Pointing the finger at us is barking up the wrong bush – if you know what I mean.' Cathy trailed off, realising she was mixing up her metaphors again.

Aisling smiled at her friend as she fetched her craft items from her bag. She had a large leather binder balanced on her knees with some parchment clipped into it. 'You know, despite all the sadness and shock of this situation, it stuns me how petty and silly some people can be,' Aisling said shyly.

The group sat with rapt attention. For Rosie, it was a gift to get some inside information on the lives of the wives of the two men who had been targeted so maliciously. She sat quietly, listening to every word.

Aisling carried on, looking more serious now, 'It's incredibly painful to think people in this town think I could have hurt my husband.' Aisling had obviously said enough. The emotion was building. She placed her binder to one side and dabbed her eyes again with a lace handkerchief. After a few moments, she reached for her tea. Her hands were trembling as she took a couple of deep gulps.

Cathy broke the silence. 'The most ridiculous thing I've heard is that apparently my friend Aisling here has been carrying on with my Sam.' Cathy giggled. 'Apparently, they were seen together at the Rocksheelan Hotel.' Cathy made air quotes around "seen". She paused and shook her head, chuckling again. 'My friend here is a bookkeeper, and my husband hasn't a clue about how to keep track of figures – except mine!' She laughed with more genuine mirth this time, and even the others joined in. Cathy was still laughing heartily even after the others had stopped, and when she eventually got her breath back, she carried on, 'Aisling was working on the accounts with him. It was me who suggested they meet up with the books over at the hotel to avoid the gossip around here. *Big* mistake.' Aisling rolled her large grey eyes. 'So, there you go, no intrigue in this neck of the woods. It's a clean slate. Nada. Nothing.' Cathy made some hand movements to show that her personal life was not a mystery.

The group nodded slowly, expressing sympathetic understanding. A chatty type, Cathy carried on, 'Poor Aisling here only lost her mammy last year. She's had a terrible time. But you're close to Marti, your brother, aren't you?'

Aisling nodded.

'Sure, Aisling was looking after Marti's kids when Gerry was found.'

The group listened avidly to Cathy while Aisling herself sat quietly. As Cathy talked, Aisling started working with some pressed flowers she had removed from an envelope. She moved them around the edge of the paper to create a border. When satisfied with the result, she carefully dabbed adhesives and pressed them deftly onto the parchment paper. She appeared absorbed in her task, and her fingers moved nimbly around the page.

Rosie watched her, mesmerised by the delicacy and care she took with her project.

Cathy had no craft items near her. She had been so busy talking and gesturing with her hands that no one had noticed. Only when she fell silent and sat there for a moment looking around her did it occur to her to fetch the materials she needed for her own work.

'Right, well, I'll go out to the car and get in my stuff.' Cathy stood up and strode purposely over to the door. The boards in the shop shook as she moved, being of a sturdy build. The door banged shut behind her. The group looked around at each other, keen to see what she would reappear with. Aisling smiled and kept her gaze on her dried flowers. Rosie was cutting out some flower shapes from felt, Marie was knitting a blanket with a floral pattern running through it, and Mary Jo was sewing up some bunting made of chintzy flowery materials.

All the ladies jumped when the door banged open again, and Cathy reappeared. The cool night air and the exertion of carrying a large plastic bin reddened her round cheeks. When she removed the lid, an earthy, damp scent of rotting organic matter filled the room. Marie blinked and wrinkled her nose.

'Peat sculptures.' Cathy declared, holding up a flower made from peat. 'I'll let this beauty dry out, and we can sell them at the May Day Fair' She looked around brightly at the group. 'What do you think, girls?' she admired her handiwork as she held the flower shape aloft. 'I think I've hit the nail on the head with his one, or I've caught two birds with one stone. I'm using a natural resource to create something, *and* I can sell it to make a bit of money for a good cause. I think it's the cherry on the iceberg...' Cathy drifted off again, looking slightly puzzled. 'Well, you get my draught!' she smiled brightly and dug her hand into the bin to pull out a big wedge of soft peat.

Rosie looked at the two women, one delicately assembling her dried flowers and the other robustly and earnestly working with her peat figures. They certainly didn't look like murderer material, although appearances could be deceptive. Rosie liked to think she had a nose for these things, which was more than she could say she had for the peat.

Rosie sniffed into her hanky and assembled her felt flowers, keeping her thoughts to herself.

CHAPTER THIRTY-FIVE

Good News

The rest of the week passed uneventfully. Sam continued to make a steady recovery but was unconscious. His wife kept vigil by his side. Aisling continued to take turns. The nurses were impressed by Cathy's stalwart friend, who turned up most days to support Cathy. Unfortunately, the nurses wouldn't allow Cathy to bring in her bin of peat to continue her craft work by his bedside, so she made do with looking at back copies of *Ireland's Own* magazine and chatting with the nurses. However, the occupational therapist welcomed Cathy into the craft room, and she was increasingly spending more time there with other patients than by her husband's side.

Dan didn't open up the second box of paperwork, but he did go back through the postcards Rosie had brought to the station. He re-read the poems more thoroughly. Even Dan had to admit that it was odd that Toddy had these in his possession. Dan put an alert out for Toddy. He was concerned for his well-being and state of mind and wanted to learn more. Just what had Toddy been up to? Toddy recalled the image being painted on the front of Sage's new shop. It was strikingly similar to the one on the postcards. What did it all mean? With irritation, Dan remembered Sergeant Kennedy was over in the station at Rocksheelan, trying to piece together what happened to Sam. Dan wanted his boss back in Erin's Glen to discuss things with him.

At St Brigid's parish office, Rosie was also patiently searching for answers to the questions on the minds of many of the Erin's Glen residents that week. Was Gerry's death just an unfortunate accident? If not, who would want to kill him and why? If it was an accident, who would go to all the trouble to arrange his body in such a fashion? When news got out about the way his body was laid out, all sorts of outlandish theories were postulated. Some older people thought it was the *Shee*, taking him as an offering. Even Rosie dismissed such stories as nonsense. And now Sam. It appeared that someone had tampered with the brakes. He had braked suddenly, probably to avoid an animal on the road – cows were always wandering the streets – and he had lost control of the car.

Rosie's mind kept returning to the visual images that dominated her thoughts. The postcards with their handwritten poems were full of supernatural threats, the old photos of people long gone, dead or moved on, and the building of the Tourist Interpretation Centre. That all seemed to have faded into the background. Thinking about these contentious plans made her think too about Fiona Fitzgerald. Where was she lately? Rosie had known Fiona for decades. Fiona was a few years younger than Rosie. Years ago, the young Fiona had run around with a set who thought they were a cut above everyone else. The photos she had looked at the previous weekend had stirred up memories from the past.

Rosie had spent the previous late afternoon browsing botanical books in the local library. She had checked out precisely what "Banshees' Bloom" was and wanted to discuss her findings with her friend, Mary Jo. She also wanted to talk to the nun about her memories going back decades. Talking through her ideas helped Rosie make sense of them. It was late on Friday morning, and Rosie decided to try ringing the school to see if she could get hold of Mary Jo. She wanted to run a few ideas past her friend, whom she knew she could trust implicitly.

Rosie was just about to pick up the phone and hesitated. She better not. She was still haunted herself by the idea that someone was listening in on her calls. Also, she had yet to find her mobile phone. Just then, she heard the front door open and close. Father Asher put his head around the door.

'Hello, stranger!' Rosie said brightly.

Father Asher slid around the door and came into the room. He looked rather sheepish as he sat down in front of Rosie.

'Yes, sorry, Rosie. I've been rather distracted this week. Truth to tell, I've been questioned by the police again. Sage has, too. The police seem very interested in us at the moment. I, err, didn't tell you the whole story when we spoke the other week.'

Rosie kept a steady, neutral gaze. She had not warmed to Sage and wasn't surprised that she, too, was a person of interest to the police.

Father Asher swept his eyes around the room and then fixed them on the box file of accounts.

Now it was Rosie's turn to look sheepish. She grinned weakly.

'Sorry, Father. I've been a bit distracted myself this week. I haven't got around to sorting through those yet.'

Father Asher shook his head and waved aside her apologies. 'Ah, right. Well, when you do go through the box, you will find plans for a retreat centre.'

Rosie looked at him without comment.

The priest continued, 'I've been thinking about opening a spiritual centre with Sage. The police found a copy of the plans in Sam's paperwork, and it alerted their interest.'

Rosie now looked annoyed with herself. A piece of the jigsaw might have been under her nose all along. Or maybe not. Rosie would need to think all this through later. For now, she focussed on what Father Asher was saying.

'It was just a proposal. I was trying to reach out to other groups, people who felt they couldn't come into the church. I think I've been very naive.'

Rosie waited.

'Anyway, the upshot of all this business is that the bishop is most unhappy with me. He disapproves of my friendship with Sage and of my ideas. Apparently, some parishioners have complained about my lack of response to Gerry's death...' Father Asher cleared his throat, and for one horrific moment, she thought he was going to cry.

Father Asher took a breath and carried on, 'Actually, the bishop is so unhappy with how I've acted here that I'm being moved out of Erin's Glen. I've got a week to pack up and say my goodbyes.'

Rosie tried not to look too pleased by this revelation. But honestly, she felt it was the first good news she'd had in weeks. She tucked her hands underneath her legs and rearranged her features into what she hoped was a shocked and sad expression.

'Oh well, Father, perhaps it's for the best.' Rosie replied with sincerity.

Chapter Thirty-Six

Making connections

That Friday afternoon, Rosie made her way homeward with her head full of loose strands. There were more questions than answers floating around. She put the box of neglected parish papers in her Mini, promising Father Asher she would at least sort them into some order over the weekend. She would have them ready for filing when she returned to work on Monday morning. On impulse, she decided to visit Mary Jo at Riverside House. She would be home from work now herself. Rosie couldn't wait. She needed to run past some theories with Mary Jo and get feedback.

Rosie pulled into the one parking space outside the house. Technically, it was a bus stop, but no one worried about that in Erin's Glen. Mary Jo was already standing at the open front door, having spotted the red Mini pull in at its odd angle.

'Come on in!' Mary Jo called out.

Rosie rushed over to the front door. 'I won't keep you, Mary Jo. I know you're probably only in the door yourself, but I wanted to chat things through.'

Mary Jo understood entirely and went through to the big kitchen with Rosie behind her.

Rosie sat at the large round table in the middle of the kitchen. Mary Jo went to put the kettle on, as was her custom when a visitor arrived, especially Rosie.

'Never worry about that.' Wholly absorbed in her thoughts, Rosie creased her brow, indicating that Mary Jo should sit down.

In truth, Mary Jo was deeply shocked by Rosie's refusal to have tea and knew something serious was happening in her mind.

'What is it?' the nun enquired as she sat opposite her friend.

'What do you know about the plant, Banshees' Bloom?' Rosie enquired abruptly.

Mary Jo considered the question. ' Well...it's a fairly harmless plant, white flowers in early spring, grows in the fields around here. Other than that, not much. Why?'

'Well, I think that's what killed Gerry.'

'Okay, but it's not poisonous', Mary Jo remonstrated.

'No, but I was speaking to Mrs Stewart in the chemists the other week. Apparently, Gerry had serious allergies. So serious that they were life-threatening. He would go into anaglypta shock if he ate certain things.'

'Anaphylactic,' Mary Jo corrected Rosie, who looked confused. 'You have anaglypta wallpaper on your walls, you numptie!'

Rosie waved her hand dismissively, 'Well, you know what I mean...anyway, he might have been allergic to this Banshees' Bloom.'

Mary Jo nodded – it was a possibility.

Mary Jo sat thinking. 'Do you think Sage is behind it? I see she is opening an herb shop in town. She must know about these things?'

Rosie considered this. 'Maybe. But I'm not convinced.'

Both ladies sat thinking.

Mary Jo was the first to break the silence. 'You know who I haven't seen for ages. Fiona Fitzgerald.'

'What makes you think of her?' Rosie asked. 'Funny, I was thinking of her, too. I found an old photo of her while sorting through some old pictures at the weekend. But sure, she's hardly been here. I lose track of where she's off to. Seeing those photos got me thinking, though… That reminds me. Are you still in touch with that wee girl you used to teach? The one who works at the Travel Agents?'

Mary Jo thought. 'Aye, Carmel. Why?'

Rosie looked at her friend and said, 'I'd be interested in asking Carmel a few questions about the travel plans of some of our neighbours.'

Just then, the phone rang in the house. Both women heard Sister Angela speak on the phone. After a brief exchange, she came into the kitchen.

'Excuse me, ladies. But that was Dan on the phone. He wants you to come round to the police station right away.

Chapter Thirty-Seven

Home

It hadn't taken long to track Toddy down. He hadn't gotten far on foot, especially carrying a wet sleeping bag and heavy spare walking boots. Many people had watched and heard him rattling along the road with his tin mug and saucepan hanging off his backpack. He had slept rough for a few nights. As Dan had suspected, Toddy had spent a couple of nights under the big old tree by the river. He looked rough. As soon as Dan had put an alert out to find him, he had been spotted on the road on the other side of Rocksheelan.

In truth, Dan was not sure what to do with him. Toddy had arrived at the station courtesy of a police officer from the next town, who was keen to get him out of the car. Toddy was in dire need of a shower and a good meal. The facilities at the station were basic but adequate. Once Toddy was washed and fed, Dan needed to ask him some questions. That was a waste of time because Toddy was a shivering wreck. He was terrified to go back to his cottage. Dan realised that Toddy was not trying to escape the police. Toddy was running away from something much more ephemeral. All Dan could ascertain was that Toddy had found Gerry's body and laid him out in a manner that would satisfy the *Shee* – at least in Toddy's poor, deranged mind. In fact, Toddy was petrified he would end up dead too. Dan gave up and decided to contact social services to get Toddy help. This had taken up most of the day. Dan was still left with his questions.

It was at the end of this frustrating day, at the end of a frustrating week, that Dan decided to swallow his pride and get on to Rosie and Mary Jo. He stood out on the step of the police station and peered up the road towards Riverside House. He spotted Rosie's car up there. Perfect. He'd get them down here and see what they had come up with over the week.

He made a quick phone call to Riverside House and left a message with one of the nuns. She promised they'd be down in a jiffy.

Dan rubbed his hands as he stood behind the front counter of the small station, waiting for the ladies' arrival. He was framing some questions in his head when the phone rang. It was Officer Finn from the Fire Brigade based just outside the town.

'Hello there, Dan, I've been trying to track down a Miss Rosie O'Reilly. Do you know her?'

'I do indeed...actually,' Dan was about to share just how well he knew Rosie. But judging by Finn's rapid questioning, he appreciated the urgency of the situation and asked, 'Why?'

Finn shot back, 'She needs to get to her home quickly. The boys are over there now putting a fire out.'

Dan rushed out the door and collided with Rosie and Mary Jo as they hurried into the police station.

When they heard his message, both women turned on their heels and shot back out the door into the Mini. As Rosie drove with shaking hands she mulled over recent unsettling events in her home – the feelings of being watched, the gate creaking open at odd hours, the smell of perfume lingering in her porch, the odd crackling and clicks on her phone – was someone trying to harm her? And if so, who?

Rosie needed to get home – fast.

Chapter Thirty-Eight

Midnight Meditations

Later that night, Dan stayed at the station. The situation in Erin's Glen was only getting more complicated, and Dan wanted to understand what was going on.

He would catch up with Rosie and learn more about the fire later. For now, all he could do was focus on office work. It was time to tackle the next box of paperwork he had avoided for quite a while. He sighed and opened up the cardboard box that had been taken from Sam's house. Dan pulled out sheets of paper and glanced at them. Most of them seemed to be accounts for the proposed Tourist Interpretation Centre. Although not superstitious, he did associate that proposal with bad luck. In fact, he had used the word 'cursed' to his wife when discussing the case. So, no wonder he avoided dealing with anything associated with it. Dan shuddered. Only for that damned place, Gerry might still be alive and Sam not fighting for his own life in hospital.

With a sigh, he pulled a ledger from the box. Blowing off a fine layer of dust, he opened it up and started pulling out invoices, proposed spends, budget allocations and details of monies received from Europe. It was the money from Europe that was going to fund the whole thing, it seemed to him. He began to assemble the disparate papers and letters. Dan had just enough grasp of the figures to see that some people in Erin's Glen were going to make a lot of money from this project. Dan began to feel angry. Very angry. Some people in this town were just parasites.

Dan knew as well as anyone that it would bring much-needed revenue into Erin's Glen, but Gerry had suffered for that. Dan turned over the pages, and a loose sheet fell out. It looked like some unrelated building plans for Fiona Fitzgerald. Dan frowned as he made sense of them. These were not related to the tourist centre. These were plans of her house and its grounds. With mounting anger, Dan saw that Fiona was getting a spa and a pool built as an extension of her home. And as far as Dan could make out, funds from the European Community were paying for it. What was Fiona Fitzgerald up to? Dan sat stroking his chin, considering the implications of this find. Sam would have known about this as it was in his possession; he would have discussed the plans with Fiona. Did Gerry find out and threaten Sam with exposure? But then, who cut the brakes in Sam's four-by-four? Did Gerry confront Fiona, and did she kill him? But how exactly? Dan shook his head in confusion. It also occurred to him that Fiona was away when Gerry was found. So, she *couldn't* have had anything to do with it. Could she?

Late that same night, Rosie was going through her own boxes of paperwork and photos. It had been an action-packed evening. Mary Jo and the other sisters at Riverside House had persuaded Rosie to stay the night with them. Before delving into the deep layer of documents, Rosie let her mind replay events from earlier that night. It had undoubtedly been a dramatic finish to the week. Upon hearing Dan's news of the fire, Mary Jo rushed back in the Mini to the bungalow with Rosie. Their first concern was Ziggy. He was alone in the house, and Rosie was frantic about the welfare of her beloved pet.

By the time they arrived, the fire brigade had doused the fire. Ziggy was in the middle of a ring of firefighters being given biscuits from a tin they kept in the fire engine cab. Catching sight of Rosie, Ziggy grabbed the last biscuit offered and sat there munching, looking mournfully at his mistress.

'Well, your wee man was the one who saved the day, you know!' A burly firefighter in yellow dungarees and hat called over to Rosie. 'His barking alerted your neighbour, who phoned us right away. We got here before there was too much damage.'

The firefighter talked with the ease of someone accustomed to such drama. He motioned for Rosie to go in, 'It looks safe enough in there, but we'll need to do a bit more of an investigation and find out how it started.'

Rosie nodded at the cheerful firefighter and bent down to greet Ziggy. She moved slowly and quietly, stunned by the reality of the fire that could have completely engulfed her home. Rosie walked into the hall she had left so casually that morning, with Mary Jo close behind her. The kitchen was the worst room affected. The rest of the house was untouched by the flames. However, the whole bungalow was suffused with the acrid smell of smoke.

Although not easily rattled, Rosie was grateful for her friend's offer of a bed for the night. Initially, she refused, but Mary Jo, usually gentle and amiable, was insistent on this occasion. Rosie relented and grabbed her overnight bag, a change of clothes and toiletries and, on impulse, picked up the small tin of old photos. She'd go back through them later.

This is what she was doing now. Rosie had retired to her room after a warm meal with the sisters and a hot bath. Ziggy was now snoozing contentedly at the foot of the bed. It was a treat for him to share a room and a bed with Rosie, and he luxuriated in the comfort.

Earlier, Rosie had brought her bag in from her car, the tin of photos, and the box of paperwork from the office. Now, at just past midnight, she was so wide awake from the dramatic events of the evening that sleep was an impossibility for her.

The house was quiet and still. The sound of Ziggy's gentle snoring was comforting. Despite the peace and comfort of her immediate surroundings, Rosie felt uneasy. Her mind ruminated over recent events. What started the fire? She considered how anxious she had been at home recently. She had the feeling that someone was watching her bungalow.

With a sudden stab of fear, accentuated by tiredness, shock and the late hour, Rosie considered the possibility that someone had tried to set her house alight. But why? Rosie sat up in bed and turned on the light. Her eye rested on the parish box file she had put in her car and later brought into her room here at Riverside House. She decided to go through its contents.

'If parish paperwork doesn't send me to sleep, nothing will,' she chuckled as she opened the box. She was sitting up in bed wearing a flannel nightie and a pink crochet bed jacket.

She perched her glasses on her nose and pulled out a handful of paperwork from the box file she had taken from the office. The bedside lamp on the table next to her gave off a soft glow. The bulb illuminated the shade with a reassuring image of Jesus with his red heart.

Rosie looked at it briefly and prayed for some mental illumination, 'Lord only knows I need all the help I can get with this mess. What on earth is going on?' she mumbled to herself as she began to clip documents together, assembling letters, invoices, bills and Mass requests into ordered piles on her bed.

One short letter caught her eye. She had seen this before amongst all the paperwork but thought nothing of it. A letter in the form of a poem written by a parishioner last year. Rosie looked closely at the handwriting. There was something remarkably familiar about it. Rosie stared at it for a few moments, then closed her eyes. An image of the poems found in Toddy's cottage came to mind. She opened her eyes and looked at the letter, which was more of a brief note in the form of a requiem poem for a deceased relative. It was penned in the same blue handwriting – a beautiful copperplate script but without the loops and slant of Sage's hand. Whoever had authored the poems had written this message.

Rosie scrabbled through the box. Yes, it was in here. A note from Sage was written on one of the note cards with the earth fairy figure on the front. Rosie looked at the letter and the note side by side. A light of recognition dawned in her eyes, and she grabbed her handbag. After searching around in the bottom of it, she unearthed the leaflet she had been given by a member of the group who seemed to be under Sage's influence. Rosie scanned the handwritten open letter addressed to Erin's Glen. It was signed by Sage. Rosie smoothed out the leaflet, the requiem poem and the note addressed to Father Asher. She laid them out side by side and spent some time studying them. She compared the formation of each letter, the size, and the angle of the writing style. In her mind's eye, she could picture the poems found in Toddy's house. It was all making sense now. She was too alert to sleep. She sat thinking quietly. Nothing could be done at this time of night except think it all through.

As soon as some light crept across the dark sky, Rosie started to get ready for the day. Ziggy stirred as Rosie got dressed. Ziggy would need a comfort break, at least, so she had a perfect reason to be up early. In truth, her mind was working fast, and she was keen to get the day started.

Rosie crept down the stairs, Ziggy behind her. The spring morning was calm and quiet. Being a Saturday, the day would take longer to get going in Erin's Glen.

Riverside House, being situated next to Abanculeen, was an ideal spot to begin a riverside walk. Ziggy ran along in front. Rosie spotted a figure in white further along the river. Ziggy had stopped in his tracks and appeared to be frozen to the spot. Sunrise was just below the horizon, and the light was murky. A mist was still hovering along the riverbank, and Rosie struggled to see what was further ahead. She could make out Ziggy's shape, sitting down, head up, ears pricked. Recognition dawned on Rosie as the figure got closer. She called Ziggy back to her side, realising that the unfriendly Madigan was accompanying the ethereal figure of Sage coming along the riverbank, out walking her dog too.

Rosie squared her shoulders and took a breath. She wasn't relishing this encounter. Ziggy sat obediently beside her, readily acquiescing to getting his lead re-attached. Rosie walked ahead, speaking in soothing tones to Ziggy, partly to reassure her pet and partly to comfort herself.

A gentle smile lit up Sage's pale face as she got closer. Madigan stood by her side, towering over Ziggy but seeming to ignore the other canine completely. Ziggy looked up at the shaggy, grey wolfhound and blinked.

'Good morning, Rosie! I see you are an early riser yourself. What a beautiful morning it is!' Sage hesitated for a second and then seized the moment. 'Rosie', she gasped.

Rosie caught the edge of anxiety in Sage's voice and looked at her full in the face, 'What is it, dear?' she asked kindly.

Sage took a breath and looked off into the distance. Rosie saw tears well up in the woman's eyes.

'I am so sorry about what has happened, but I *am* innocent. I want you to know that.' Sage gazed intently into Rosie's eyes as one tear slowly rolled down the taller woman's cheek. A woman of few words, Sage then tightened her hold on Madigan's lead and strode along the riverbank.

Rosie stepped aside as Sage glided past, muttering a farewell out of polite habit. Rosie was a little perplexed by her encounter with the mysterious Sage. She stood for a moment, looking after the tall woman in white accompanied by her leggy hound. Ziggy whimpered and pulled on the lead, and they continued on their way.

The smell of freshly baked bread brought them both back toward the town. Super Quinn, the local supermarket, had a bakery on site, and Rosie decided to pop in to buy some fresh bread to take back for breakfast. She was tying Ziggy's lead up outside when Trish, her hairdresser, shouted over from across the street.

Rosie waited while Trish rushed over, keen to speak with her client and friend.

'Rosie, I heard about the fire. God, are you alright? You must have had a terrible shock! I heard wee Ziggy here was the star!'

Trish earnestly surveyed Rosie and Ziggy, and once she was satisfied that they were both in good health, she continued with astounding rapidity.

'Have you heard the latest?' Trish was obviously in a rush, so Rosie shook her head quickly while Trish gushed out the latest update on events in Erin's Glen.

'Well, my sister has just been on the phone. Her husband was at the match last weekend.'

Rosie's attention was fixed on Trish, who was referring to the football match that Sam had attended before his car accident. 'She told me that Marti Cassidy – you know Marti, Gerry's brother-in-law – has been arrested in Rocksheelan. He was seen tampering with Sam's car. Anyway, I need to fly. See you over at the salon, Rosie, cheerio for now!' Trish raised her hand and ran across to her flat above her hair salon.

Rosie had lost her appetite for bread and decided to return quickly to Riverside House. She needed to talk with Mary Jo and sort out her chaotic thoughts.

Ziggy protested mildly at the confusion, whining with disappointment as they left the shop without any treats. But he trotted along faithfully with his mistress, only occasionally glancing up at her sullenly.

The nuns were already up and preparing breakfast when Rosie got back to Riverside House.

'Ah, there she is!' Sister Angela called cheerfully. 'And the wee man himself. The wee hero – who wants a sausage?' Ziggy's mood brightened as he was presented with a plate covered in chopped-up sausages.

'Well, we don't usually have these treats at breakfast, but as we have visitors...' Sister Angela was now filling up the humans' plates with sausages, bacon, fried eggs, and soda farls. 'I hope you're hungry, girls!'

The two other elderly nuns looked slightly overwhelmed, but a familiar voice called in from the hall, 'Certainly am, bring it on!' Mary Jo bounded in, fresh-faced from an early morning jog. She caught Rosie's eye. She had clearly heard the latest news concerning who had cut Sam's brakes, too. Both women understood each other without having to say a word.

Rosie had now worked up an appetite and did justice to her plateful. Ziggy disgraced himself by constantly asking for seconds and more, which the nuns readily supplied.

Rosie was about to open her mouth to tell Ziggy off for his greed when the phone rang. Sister Angela scuttled off to answer the phone.

'Ah, good morning, Officer Finn. Yes, she is indeed. I'll go and fetch her.'

Angela popped her head around the door. 'It's for you, Rosie. Officer Finn from the fire brigade. He tried you at home, and when he couldn't get you in, he thought you might be here.'

A look of panic passed over her face. Rosie was already on her feet and making her way to the phone. She picked up the receiver.

'Good morning…yes I'm fine…no worries…oh thank God for that.'

There was a pause while Rosie took in the information Officer Finn was imparting.

'Mmm, I see. Right, you are. Ah, sure I know, yes indeed…' Officer Finn was obviously speaking at length. Rosie's expression changed from curious to sheepish.

Mary Jo sat in the kitchen with the other three nuns, overhearing Rosie's end of the conversation. Ziggy was at Angela's feet, looking between her and his mistress out in the hall by the phone.

'Right-o, well, you know…' Rosie laughed lightly, trailing off. 'Thanks, officer. Bye now, bye, bye…bye.' Rosie put the receiver down quickly. She hesitated before returning to the kitchen.

Mary Jo sat with a stern but playful look on her face. Her brow furrowed, but the corners of her mouth were upturned in a teasing smirk. 'What have you been doing, you numpty?' she asked her friend lightly. The others looked a bit perplexed.

Rosie was slightly flushed and hesitated before she spoke, 'Well, it would seem that the cause of the fire in my kitchen was my cupcake maker.'

'Oh dear.' Mary Jo said, shaking her head.

'I swear that thing has been malfunctioning. I will write to the manufacturer and complain...' Rosie trailed off, realising that her protestations were falling on deaf ears.

'Rosie, just don't even *try* using the gadgets. You're safer with the old range; you know where you are with that,' Mary Jo chided.

'Right, well, it's put my mind at rest. At least I know it wasn't foul play,' Rosie said, beginning to stack the plates, indicating that the topic was closed.

'Ah well, as long as you're alright, no harm done.' Sister Angela stood up and began clearing the dishes away.

The two older nuns drifted off out of the kitchen. Before they retired to the study to work on their scarf. Sister Eileen giggled, 'We are knitting the world's longest scarf.' When Rosie looked blank, her companion, Sister Maureen, elaborated, 'We are raising money for the missions. We're getting sponsored. It'll bring much publicity to a good cause!' The two elderly nuns, slightly bent over and linking arms with each other for support, shuffled off in their slippers to do a bit of extreme knitting.

Sister Angela insisted on washing up. Rosie and Mary Jo dried up quickly. Angela went to a drawer on the enormous old sideboard and rummaged through kitchen utensils, scraps of paper, pens, string, and clothes pegs. 'Ah, here it is!' she produced a tatty-looking jotter. My master plans!' she grinned. 'I'm putting together a recipe book to sell in the parish. It's called *Heavenly Eats*.'

Unbudded, she read aloud some of the recipes: *Blessed Beetroot Salad, Loaves and Fishes starter bowl, Angel's Hair Pasta Salad.*' She looked up from her jotter and could tell Rosie and Mary Jo were politely waiting for her to finish. 'Right, so I'll get off then.' Slightly crestfallen about their lack of enthusiasm for her project, Angela scuttled off to the study to join Eileen and Maureen.

As the door closed behind her and silence descended on the kitchen, both women sighed in relief. So much was going on in both of their minds, and they desperately needed the opportunity to talk it all through privately.

Mary Jo sat serenely at the table, her hands clasped in front of her, waiting for Rosie to start. In truth, Rosie hardly knew where to start. She sat for a moment, looking ahead. She tapped the table with both hands and began with the latest news.

'Right, well, I assume you've heard the news this morning?'

'Aye,' Mary Jo confirmed she had heard about Marti Cassidy being accused of tampering with Sam's brakes.

Rosie continued, 'Now, I had the strangest dream last night. I dreamed about Gerry. I thought he was standing outside the chemist, as clearly as I can see you now. He opened his jacket, and inside, I could see his heart, red and bright like a light. He was putting his hands in his pocket, and I woke up when he took his hand out. I thought he would show me something; it was the strangest thing.'

Mary Jo considered this. 'Well, he died of a heart attack, but I wonder what he was going to show you.' Mary Jo pondered this, considering it a perfectly reasonable line of inquiry.

'The other thing I was thinking about is this...' Rosie fished about her pocket and pulled out the photos and the note she had been looking at the night before.

Mary Jo studied the note, 'This looks like the same writing as——'

'Exactly!' Rosie knew what her friend was going to say. Sage signed the note. The apparent similarity to the handwriting the poems were penned in was striking. It looked like Sage had written the poems. Mary Jo turned over the notecard and spotted the same picture.

'So, do you think Sage was putting Toddy up to all of this?' Mary Jo sat with her hand to her mouth, thinking.

Rosie produced the photos: 'I found these recently. I'd forgotten all about these. Also, I was listening to The Golden Oldies Show on the radio last Sunday, and it brought it all back.'

Mary Jo took the first photo. A young couple is sitting on a patch of grass, the fairy ring in the background with the oak tree at the top. Both were smiling. The young woman sat primly, a vast, chequered skirt covering her knees, her hands clasped around them. A high-necked white blouse with a frilly ruff completed her outfit. The young man reclined beside her. His head was nestled against the side of her arm. He wore loose trousers and an open-necked shirt. They both looked relaxed and happy, and even in the black and white photo, their faces glowed with the light from the sun and their exuberant youth.

Mary Jo studied the picture, 'I know who that is. That's a young Fiona Fitzgerald. But who is that she's with?'

'That's Cosmos.' Came Rosie's reply.

Mary Jo looked blank, 'Cosmos?'

'Yes, the brother of Cornelius Quinn. He's a Don or a Professor or something high-falootin' in Ancient Celtic History, with a specialist in artefacts. He left Erin's Glen years ago. He studied at Trinity in Dublin and then went over the water.'

'Ah, right so.'

'I was thinking Fiona might still be in contact with Cosmos...' Rosie was still looking intently at the photo.

Mary Jo continued, do you think Fiona is still in touch with him and has orchestrated all this to get at some artefacts in the fairy ring?' Mary Jo considered other options. 'Or perhaps it's Cornelius. Do you think he's been behind all this to get at something up there? I did see him up there with that metal detector. I suppose it's a possibility. But why murder Gerry? And if he *was* murdered, why go to all the trouble of laying his body out like that?'

Rosie sat and listened. It always helped to talk things through like this with her friend and confidante.

'Wait!' Mary put up her index finger. 'Was he trying to set up Sage, do you think?

'I think you are getting closer, Mary Jo. I think someone was trying to frame Sage – but it wasn't Fiona, Cosmos, or Cornelius.'

Her eyes glittering, Rosie revealed another more recent picture stuck behind the old photo they had been examining.

'Now, look at this!' she said triumphantly.

Ziggy gave a loud bark.

Chapter Thirty-Nine

One Year Later

It had been an eventful twelve months in Erin's Glen. The law had taken its course and justice was done. Almost one year after Rosie and Mary Jo had been looking at those old photos of couples from the past, a national news programme, *Spotlight*, aired an episode that focused on the mystery Rosie had unravelled. Rosie invited Mary Jo to her house for an early dinner to celebrate their sleuthing achievements. Mary Jo said she would bring fish and chips, and then they could settle down to watch the *Spotlight* special. The TV show's current affairs and news program was doing an episode on the murder in the fairy ring, and the two women didn't want to miss it.

As Rosie bustled about the kitchen, sorting plates and cutlery, she recalled how those old photos had alerted her. It was not the photo of Fiona and Cosmos but the photo of two teenagers from the 1970s that helped Rosie begin to piece everything together and work out exactly what had happened.

Mary Jo arrived as promised, bearing their fish and chip suppers. Both sat eating quietly when the program came on. The television presenter spoke while familiar scenes of the locality flashed up on the screen.

'There have been strange happenings in this small rural town. It all seems to have started last year with proposals to build a tourist centre on the site of the fairy ring, close to Erin's Glen town.'

The segment went on to rehash how Gerry's body was found. Photos of Gerry, Sam Bazley, and Fiona Fitzgerald flashed up on the screen, all of whom had a stake in the building of the centre. Some time was spent on the scandal that came to light. Fiona Fitzgerald was creaming off money intended for the creation of the centre and using some of it to construct her own spa and pool. Sam Bazley, the builder, was in cahoots with the skullduggery. Mary Jo and Rosie sat in rapt attention, slowly munching on their fish and chips as Ziggy watched them, drooling. In the fading spring light of early evening, the light from the screen flashed across their faces.

The TV presenter continued:

'...it seemed that the councillor had discovered the financial irregularity. He was seen by a local bookstore owner confronting Sam Bazley.' At this point, a picture of Deirdre flashed up as the witness. 'However, the tale then took a bizarre turn. A local unemployed man with mental health issues fled his home, and police discovered links between him, the builder, and the leader of a local cult.'

Some old news footage with Toddy in the background was shown, followed by a picture of Sage.

At this point, Rosie interrupted, 'That's a cheek. We found the links! As if the police found those poems in Toddy's house. Sure, that was us!'

Mary Jo silenced her, and they continued listening and eating.

'Cryptic poems that appeared to be penned by the cult leader were found in Toddy's home. Sam Bazley's jacket was also found in the cottage belonging to Toddy O'Raw, linking the builder close to the site where the body was found. So just what were the connections between Gerry, Sam, Fiona, Toddy, and Sage? There were rumours in the town that Sam was having an affair with Gerry's wife, Aisling, but the theory that Aisling had somehow been involved in her husband's death was squashed when it transpired that Aisling was thirty miles away caring for her nieces and nephews in her brother's home.

In addition, Aisling's alleged lover, Sam, was himself the victim of an attack on his life. His brakes were tampered with, and his subsequent car accident resulted in the builder ending up in a critical condition in hospital. A witness subsequently came forward, informing police that they had seen Aisling's brother, Marti Cassidy, tamper with Sam's brakes. It would seem Marti took this action in revenge for the death of his brother-in-law. Marti believed that Sam had caused Gerry's death and made his sister, Aisling, a widow.

So, it's been a tangled web of deceit here in the glen by the fairy ring. Let's talk to some locals for their opinion on events.' The reporter turned to speak to Mrs Blaney, who had been waiting patiently, her eyes fixed on the camera as she gripped her handbag in front of her.

At this point, Rosie switched the volume down. Mary Jo and Rosie needed to take a break to reflect on how the story unfolded. They could watch Mrs Blaney anytime spouting her opinion; they didn't need to watch her on television. Even with no sound, it was apparent that a few other locals declined to comment, putting up their hoods, pulling caps down, and walking off. Not everyone in Erin's Glen wanted to be in the limelight.

After Mrs Blaney and Mrs Kirkpatrick had their say, the TV presenter returned to how the truth had unfolded.

'It was the input of this local woman.' Rosie smiled shyly when her photo flashed on the screen with her name underneath. The commentator continued, 'Rosie O'Reilly, a local parish secretary, had questioned a chemist in the town about the medications Gerry was taking. The councillor had some severe life-threatening allergies that, left untreated, could bring on a heart attack. Gerry had been found with an empty bottle of his medication in his pocket. Rosie realised these allergies and the empty medication bottle were a key aspect of the case. She linked this knowledge with instructions found at Toddy's house to prepare a brew of Banshees' Bloom and give it to Gerry. However, no trace of Banshee's Bloom was found in Toddy's cottage. Also, it emerged that the instructions, written in the form of a poem, were on the face of it, written by Sage, the cult leader. So, did Sage write the poems on the postcards? She had invited Gerry to meet her to discuss the new building. A note from Sage was found in Gerry's pocket. It also transpired that Sage had plans herself to build an eco-retreat, as a joint project with the local priest no less. Was Sage ruthless enough to murder Gerry, who supported the tourist centre, which she opposed? Did she give Gerry a lethal concoction? Did she persuade Toddy to do it? And if Toddy didn't give Gerry the Banshees' Bloom, then who did? More significantly, *how*? How *did* Gerry ingest a substance that was so lethal for him? Join us after the break to find out.'

Rosie was dismissive of her sleuthing fame and said casually, 'Ah, we might as well switch it off now. We know the rest of the story anyway. Sure, I'm taping it. We can watch it tomorrow.' Rosie switched off the television set and pointed to her new VHS recorder, which had a red light on. Mary Jo thought the blinking crimson button looked hopeful.

'Well, it didn't look good for Sage for a while, I must admit.' Mary Jo reflected.

'Yes, it's just as well I nagged the police. That old photo alerted me.'

Rosie was referring to the image captured a generation later, in the 1970s. The picture of a young, skinny Sam and a youthful Aisling Cassidy as she was before her marriage to Gerry.

'Yes, it was *that* photo. It brought it all back. Sam and Aisling were a bit of an item. But Sam went away to work down south and met Cathy. I don't think he was ever serious about Cathy, poor girl, but it transpired she fell pregnant, and they had to get married quickly. Cathy told me about her unexpected pregnancy during the craft group. God love her, she was telling me what a good man he is. But that got me thinking. Apparently, Aisling married Gerry soon after. Gerry was a lot older and had done well for himself. I suppose Aisling thought he was a good catch. But it would seem Aisling and Sam never settled into their new relationships. Who knows how long Aisling and Sam had been cooking this up? Years perhaps.' Rosie shook her head.

Mary Jo picked up the threads here. 'What amazed me was *how* she did it – *how* devious it was.'

'Aye. But she didn't factor in how she can't control other people. She might have planned it all out, but people have free will. You can't always plan how they will act or react.' Rosie interjected.

'True enough.' Mary Jo agreed.

Rosie sat shaking her head. The two women were still processing the recent memories triggered by the television programme, and it was therapeutic to talk them all through.

Rosie continued, 'Yes, Aisling didn't factor in that Toddy would take it all so seriously. Poor Toddy, in his demented state, found Gerry's body and thought he'd present him as an offering to the *Shee*. He was the one who made all that effort to lay the body out with the sheet, water, feathers, salt, and stones. If Gerry had just dropped down with a heart attack and just been left there, it wouldn't have aroused so much suspicion. Aisling overplayed her hand there, although it did add to the impression that Sage was responsible for Gerry's death, I suppose. So, I guess Aisling wasn't too bothered. It took the focus away from her. What does seem so heartless to me is deliberately frightening Toddy with those poems and implicating him. She must have got Sam to knock around the house, scaring that poor critter. It also wouldn't surprise me if Sam planted some Banshee's Bloom in the cottage, but Toddy probably put the foul-smelling stuff on the fire.'

Mary Jo agreed and continued, 'She also didn't factor in that her brother Marti would take against Sam and blame him for the death of his brother-in-law. Little did he know his sister was planning on running off with Sam.'

Both women sat shaking their heads.

Mary Jo wrinkled her brow, 'What puzzled me was Marti's failure to connect Sam with Aisling. They must have hidden it well.'

Rosie started counting back on her fingers, calculating how old Aisling's youngest brother would have been back in the 70s. Confident of her calculations, she confirmed, 'Sure, Marti wasn't much more than a baby when Sam and Aisling were running about together as teenagers. He wouldn't have remembered. Marti and Gerry got on well. Gerry confided in Marti. Marti must have thought Sam was trying to cover up his financial shenanigans and assumed that Sam had killed his brother-in-law because Gerry had got wind of what Sam was up to. As far as Marti was concerned, Sam had made his sister a widow, and he was getting revenge on behalf of Aisling and his brother-in-law, who he looked up to.'

After a pause, Mary Jo commented, 'Yes, and of course, Aisling was doing the accounts for Sam, or so they said, and that provided an excuse for their meetings. Aisling made all this effort to be with Sam. It's all wasted now. That's three men's lives gone or ruined because of her.' The usually mild Mary Jo was breathing heavily and looking red in the face.

After a moment, Mary Jo recovered enough to remember Rosie was supposed to be recording the rest of the programme. With some well-founded doubt about Rosie's video recording abilities, she asked, 'Shall we just watch the last wee bit of the programme?'

'Aye, go on then.' Rosie snapped the television back on.

The assured voice of the television presenter was still going: '...Rosie spotted the similarity of the handwriting the poems were written in with other paperwork she had access to. She also detected the differences in how individual letters were formed. Indeed, the eagle-eyed sleuth spotted some inconsistencies in the handwriting that would indicate the person who penned the poem was trying to *copy* the cult leader's handwriting. Sage had written an open letter to the residents of Erin's Glen, so her handwriting style was public knowledge and could have been copied by anyone in the town. Miss O'Reilly's position as parish secretary in the town gave her access to paperwork from which she deduced exactly *who* had copied Sage's handwriting and *who* produced the poems. Rosie O'Reilly tipped off the police about her suspicions about Aisling. After finding out about Gerry's allergies, Rosie questioned a local chemist. The amateur detective deduced that Aisling had tampered with Gerry's medication. Then, as a result of finding an old photograph depicting Sam and Aisling as a young couple in years gone by, she also realised that Sam and Aisling must have rekindled their relationship. On a hunch, she concluded they would most likely have plans to flee Erin's Glen.'

Next, some footage of the Travel Agents, where Mary Jo's ex-pupil, Carmel, worked, flashed up.

The commentary continued: 'Rosie questioned a contact at Rocksheelan Travel Agents, who confirmed that one-way tickets to Australia had been booked in the names of Sam Bazley and Aisling Cassidy. Staff at the travel agents in the town thirty miles away from Erin's Glen had not recognised Mrs Macauley's birth name: Cassidy. They had not linked the booking with this case until Rosie questioned them. So, it was obvious Aisling and Sam had hatched a plan to be together and leave Erin's Glen forever. In addition, one of Aisling's fingerprints was found on the cards with the poems written on them. This information gave the police justification to search Aisling's house.'

A picture of the house Aisling and Gerry had shared appeared next on the screen. The commentary continued, 'Aisling was a tidy housekeeper, but she had missed one tiny item at the back of a kitchen drawer – a small capsule. Also, minute traces of the plant Banshees' Bloom were found in her kitchen. It appeared she was using her kitchen as a makeshift chemist. Aisling had usually collected her husband's allergy medication from the chemists in Erin's Glen. The treacherous wife had seized this opportunity to tamper with her husband's medicine. She knew he was extremely allergic to the local plant, Banshees' Bloom. With the cold heart of a murderer, she had made up capsules containing dried Banshees' Bloom. She had used a bottle of medicine fetched from the chemist, replaced the bona fide allergy medication with one homemade capsule, and left it for him to take on the day she was absent – the fateful day Sage had invited Gerry to meet her on the fairy ring. Aisling knew he would go up to the hill fort in response to the note. To cover herself, Aisling had arranged to care for her nieces and nephews in Rocksheelan, miles away from the scene of her husband's death. Not only was Gerry *not* getting the drug he needed to ward off a life-threatening allergic reaction, but Aisling was giving him the very substance that would hasten his death. Gerry died of a heart attack brought on by an allergic reaction to Banshee's Bloom.'

The scene on the screen switched to Toddy's ramshackle cottage. The reporter continued, 'Aisling took advantage of a local man with mental health issues, placing hand-written poems containing references to the plant to explain the substance that would be found in Gerry's system. She concocted a scenario in which it would appear that Sage was manipulating Toddy. Gerry's widow knew Sage would have many witnesses from within her group. However, implicating Toddy added a dimension to the case that meant even if Sage had an alibi, the blame could be pinned on the isolated Toddy. Sage would be in the frame as the arch-manipulator, seemingly controlling Toddy. Aisling, a talented calligrapher, copied Sage's handwriting. A jotter in Aislings home had indented writing on unused sheets, indicating her efforts to practice penning the poems in Sage's handwriting. A blue fountain pen in her home matched the ink with which the poems were penned. It would also appear that Aisling had forged the note from Sage, luring Gerry up to the hill fort.'

A photo of Aisling flashed up. It was an unflattering police mug shot.

'So, there you have it. A sorry ending to a tragic tale of old romances, regrets, murder, and intrigue.'

Rosie got up quickly and silenced the television set, switching the volume button to mute. A weather presenter mimed the movement of something across Ireland, and it wasn't rain for a change. Mary Jo smiled at all the sunny symbols the presenter stuck on the map.

'Right now, let's see if this thing recorded all that.' Rosie put her glasses on and knelt to peer at the VHS tape recorder on a shelf below the television set. With a frown, she pressed a few buttons, and the screen was filled with white fuzzy snow and a hissing sound. A picture zig-zagged horizontally across the screen. 'Ah, this is it; it's recorded!' Rosie shouted triumphantly.

A chaotic pub scene came into focus. Exuberant cheering and clapping filled the room. The screen split in two with a subtitled ribbon moving along the bottom, informing watchers that this was *'Paddy's Peculiar Pub Quiz: Guinness Records Section.'* Two contestants appeared on either side of the screen. On one side, a large elderly lady was seated at a table with a pile of potatoes in front of her, and on the other side, a diminutive middle-aged man was performing a rapid jig on a bar stool. The lady was furiously peeling potatoes, and the subtitle, *'How many spuds can she peel in a minute?'* was running below her image. The middle-aged man was dancing with a fixed, determined grin, and underneath his picture, the subtitle read, *'How long can he jig on the stool?'* Raucous studio laughter, cheers and shouts filled the room.

Rosie stepped back in shock to look at the screen, her brow wrinkled in confusion. '*That's* not the news.'

Ziggy wiggled his eyebrows, and Mary Jo just smiled.

CHAPTER FORTY

Revelations, Reunions and Retreats

At last, a year later, May Day arrived. The official celebrations had been cancelled the year before due to the murder of Gerry Macauley. Everyone in the town agreed it would be respectful to pause the festivities until the case was settled.

This May Day, Erin's Glen residents and visitors woke to a blue sky covered in a lattice of lacy white clouds and a warm breeze. Twelve months had passed since all the drama of Aisling Macauley's arrest for the murder of her husband and Aisling was behind bars. Her brother Marti *had* tampered with Sam's brakes, so he was also in custody. Marti had the correct impression that Sam was involved somehow in the murder of Gerry, his brother-in-law. However, he was unaware of Sam's relationship with his sister and must have bitterly regretted his misplaced sibling loyalty. Of course, Fiona had employed a top-notch lawyer and insisted her apparent financial irregularities were all just a dreadful misunderstanding. Despite this, Fiona had not managed to avoid losing her liberty. Still, she continued to protest her innocence and spent her days writing letters to her political contacts, asking for their support in demanding she be released.

But today was not a day to worry about the consequences of such despicable actions. It was a day for merriment, fun, and answers to other less pressing but puzzling questions. The community would be gathered together to celebrate an ancient festival. During the conversations, reunions, and chance encounters, mysteries that had baffled some of the inhabitants of Erin's Glen over the past few months would be solved.

Dan decided to go for an early morning cycle ride through the town. He felt more relaxed these days, knowing that Erin's Glen was a safe and happy place to live again. He was up and out before the day started, but as he pedalled past Rainbow Row, there were signs of preparations for the day's festivities. He passed Mrs Blaney's B&B. The *No Vacancies* sign was up. He caught sight of Mrs B standing by a table at the front window, teapot in her hands as she topped up guests' teacups. No doubt, she also topped up news of recent events. He looked over to O'Hara's Hair and Beauty and spotted a few young women getting prettied up for the parade later. Super Quinn was open and doing a roaring trade in gee-gaas for the big day. He spotted various people coming out with balloons, ribbons, streamers, flowers, and supplies for picnics. It was the town's tradition to open celebrations by the clock tower by Rainbow Row. They would then parade up to the fairy ring. Once they were all assembled at the top, folk would attach May Day wishes to the oak tree. Dozens of brightly coloured ribbons would be fluttering in the breeze. Then, there would be picnics, dancing and socialising around the fort. Traditionally, Erin's Glen residents believed that the little people loved all the singing and dancing, so it was always a carefree gathering.

Dan pulled up outside Cornelius' antique shop, Quinn's Curiosities, and spotted Cornelius putting up a sign in the window. Seeing the police officer stop by the window, Cornelius came out to greet him.

'Good morning, officer.'

Dan didn't respond immediately as he was reading the brief typed sign:

Mobile phone found in this shop. Please enquire within.

Cornelius followed Dan's gaze. 'Ah, yes, I found that phone way back last year when all that business was going on concerning poor Mr Macaulay. I wasn't sure what to do about it and completely forgot about it. I didn't want to bother you about such trivia at the time, when you had so many more important matters to deal with.'

Dan smiled and nodded, 'Well, I think this mystery is an easy one to solve. Speak to Rosie!' Dan pushed off on his bike, Cornelius looking slightly perplexed.

'I will do indeed,' he called back, muttering under his breath, 'Yes, she seems to solve all the mysteries around here.'

Dan cycled past Reid and Wright's Stationers, Bookshop and Café and waved at Marie and Deirdre, who were setting up tables outside the shop. Ready to take advantage of passing trade.

Dan continued up past Riverside House, where the nuns were treating Rosie and Ziggy to breakfast inside. Rosie had the day off, and Mary Jo had suggested they come down early into the town to celebrate the special day. Rosie had moved back into her bungalow soon after the fire there. It was all good once the kitchen was cleaned and a little redecorating was done.

Sister Angela had taken charge of the cooking again, and her efforts were all well received, especially by her new best friend, Ziggy, who looked up at her adoringly. The nun tutted when she dropped some food on the floor as she cleared away the plates from the table. Ziggy was on to it as quick as a flash.

'He's better than the Hoover. Good lad clearing up there!' Angela praised the curly-haired hound as he licked his lips appreciatively.

Rosie suddenly delved into her handbag. 'Well, as it seems to be a day to clear up what's been happening around here, I brought this to show you,' she said, passing a letter to Mary Jo.

The nun scanned it while Angela fussed over Ziggy.

The letter was from Telecom Éireann, the national phone company. Mary Jo absorbed the contents, folded it up, and handed it back to Rosie, merriment dancing in her blue eyes. She smiled indulgently at her sleuthing friend and confirmed with her what she had just read: 'So, there was a fault on the line. No phone tapping in Erin's Glen last year, then.'

Rosie nodded, slightly embarrassed by her overreaction.

'Well, let's be thankful for small mercies.' Mary Jo fixed her gaze on Rosie and then asked, 'I suppose there were no intruders in your house either?'

Rosie nodded, 'No, I was just getting a bit nervous.'

'The creaking gate?' The nun queried.

'Some WD40 fixed that.' Rosie fumbled in her bag again, 'And I got to the bottom of the perfume smell in my porchway.' She brandished an Avon catalogue.

'Ah, "*Avon Calling*," not the *Shee* then!' Mary Jo teased.

'No, apparently Trish was doing Avon for a while as the hairdressing went quiet. She wasn't doing it for long. But the other day, I was in the salon, and she was reeking of the same perfume I had smelled on my porch last year. That's when I realised. I must have been getting a bit jumpy.'

Mary Jo looked at the catalogue. Rosie pointed to the perfume bottle pictured in the catalogue, 'Trish still had some catalogues and a sample of the perfume.'

Mary Jo laughed at the scent's name: '*Enchanted*! Were you tempted to get some?'

Rosie pursed her lips, shook her head, and tutted by way of reply. Rosie returned the catalogue to her bag, indicating the topic was closed.

'Ah well, it was understandable in the circumstances. Everyone was feeling a bit jumpy last year with all that *Shee* business going on,' Mary Jo commented kindly.

'Yes, another thing that made me jumpy last year was seeing Sage out at night for the first time. That was before I even knew her. Gave me the fright of my life, she did.' Rosie put her hand to her heart as she recalled what she thought was an apparition at the time.

'Oh aye, I see her out and about at all hours. She likes being out in the moonlight, she tells me. Being so pale, too much sun doesn't agree with her. Not that we get that much sun here! She's an unusual woman, but sure, it takes all sorts. I hear she's moved into a flat over her shop now in Rainbow Row. Her group have all wandered off now. I believe they are protesting at a site over in England with that Swampy fella.' Mary Jo folded her hands as she considered the recent turn of events.

After a few seconds, Rosie moved on to another topic and asked, 'What's happening with Toddy?'

With her sing-song voice, Angela piped up, 'Well, I'm pleased to say Toddy is doing well. As you know the police didn't press charges for his interference with Gerry's remains. God rest his soul and all the souls of the faithful departed...' The four nuns blessed themselves in unison without taking a breath.

Sister Angela carried on the story of Toddy's recuperation. She had been in touch with the Sisters of Mercy, who ran a sanitorium on the coast. He was doing well. Sister Angela reflected on the situation momentarily and commented, 'Poor Toddy didn't mean any harm. He thought he was appeasing the fairies. Sam had been knocking around the cottage, terrorising poor Toddy into thinking the *Shee* were after him because he hadn't protected the fairy ring. Poor Toddy thought Sam was his friend. Sam would go into the cottage to talk to Toddy, winding him up with stories about the wee folk and planting those poems there. Unforgivable to take advantage of a poor soul like that. I know I'm a nun, but I struggle to feel much mercy for *that* woman.' Sister Angela was referring to Aisling, of course.

No one else mentioned Sam, who was still in a hospital bed. The prognosis didn't look good.

Angela paused here to make loud tutting noises and shake her head disapprovingly. The others joined in with similar expressions. She continued, 'Anyway, I've organised a team of cleaners to go into the cottage and get it all tidied up for him. Cathy, Sam's wife, has arranged for some builders to go and make some repairs too.' Angela's eyes twinkled behind her wire-rimmed glasses.

'Ah, that's great news.' Rosie nodded enthusiastically, heartened to hear the community banding together to help the isolated man.

'Yes, hopefully, he'll return home when he's all better. He's still having a few wee episodes.' Angela left it there. A respectful silence descended.

Mary Jo shook her head sadly, 'I've heard Sam is still in a bad way. Permanent brain damage, the doctors say, but Cathy still goes up to the hospital every day, despite everything that has happened.'

Even the other nuns were astounded at Cathy's generosity of spirit.

Rosie shifted in her chair and felt the need to put them right. 'Well, yes, she *does* go up there every day, but she is helping the occupational therapist at the hospital.'

The others looked a bit blank.

'She's running sessions on peat sculpture-making. She's starting her own business, teaching and selling her creations. And speaking of creations, I've heard Hayden, Cornelius' nephew, is making a BBC documentary about the folklore of Erin's Glen.'

Marie had kept in touch with the young man. She had told Rosie that Hayden had left Erin's Glen quickly, as he needed to talk urgently with the BBC producer, considering everything that had happened. Cornelius wanted to keep it quiet at the time in case it didn't go ahead. However, it had been produced despite the tragic events. Marie had stayed connected with the young man who had returned to England and kept Rosie updated on the progress of his project.

The sound of a crackling PA system drifted down the street.

'Right, well, we'd better be making a move if we're going to join in the celebrations,' Rosie stood up. Ziggy, usually up on his feet in a flash, was slow to move. He had draped himself across Angela's feet. She just chuckled and gave him a gentle nudge with her foot.

Angela walked with them to the front door, dressed in her habit, floral pinny, and sheepskin slippers. She eyed Rosie merrily and said, 'Well, Rosie, have you heard from your old boss?'

Rosie nodded, 'Aye, Father Asher is doing well. The bishop sent him to run a retreat centre in the city. He loves it. It's right up his street, apparently.'

Angela nodded in understanding and whispered, 'He wasn't really parish priest material, was he?'

Mary Jo cut the conversation short. She wanted to get on, so she opened the substantial old door to show it was time to leave.

When the solid door creaked open, sunlight dazzled Rosie, Ziggy, and Mary Jo. The hallway's interior gloom contrasted with the bright spring day. Outside on the street, the folk group was getting warmed up. Stalls were set out along the street. The road was closed to traffic, and the buildings along Rainbow Row were festooned with bunting and streamers.

The trio strolled along in the sunshine, admiring stalls and browsing the items on sale. Mary Jo and Rosie stopped by a stall dedicated to raising funds for the local girls' school where Mary Jo worked. The items they had lovingly worked on in the craft group were on sale. A selection of felt flower brooches made by Rosie herself. Marie and Deirdre created a few small, knitted blankets with a floral motif. Mary Jo and Rosie glanced at the small, framed poems, penned in blue ink in a distinctive copperplate style, each decorated with dried flowers. They knew who had made those, but both ladies kept a discreet silence.

They had nearly walked the whole street, and Rosie spotted Sage standing outside her shop, watching the festivities and waving at passersby. She looked relaxed in a white tunic and baggy trousers, her pale hair in two plaits on either side of her face.

Rosie went over to her, 'How's business?' she asked.

'Grand!' Sage returned.

The two women regarded each other much more warmly. Rosie realised that Sage meant well and that her earlier reserve was due to shyness. Growing up in Erin's Glen, Rosie wasn't used to reserved people. Sage and Rosie were very different women from different generations and regions of Ireland, but they had grown accustomed to each other over the year and grown closer. Rosie looked in the window of Sage's shop. Peat statues were on sale. A little card showed that the artist was Cathy Bazley. Rosie smiled to herself.

Sage followed Rosie's gaze, 'Actually, the shop is doing so well that I've abandoned my initial idea of the eco-retreat centre. I wouldn't have the time.' Sage tickled Ziggy behind the ears. He looked around nervously. 'Don't worry,' Sage laughed. Madigan is out the back with Mac.'

'Mac?' Rosie enquired.

'Yes. "Mac" – short for McKenzie – I've got another wolfhound puppy. Isn't that exciting?' Sage clasped her hands like a child at Christmas.

'Great!' Rosie chimed back without enthusiasm. She looked around, but Mary Jo was gone. After a moment, she spotted her talking to Cornelius across the road. She made a hasty retreat before Madigan appeared with Mac and trotted over to join Mary Jo and Cornelius.

Mary Jo turned around smiling. Cornelius spoke first, 'I believe I might have something belonging to you!'

Rosie gasped, 'Where did you find that?' she looked stunned to see her mobile phone again after all this time.

'In the shop. You must have left it behind when you popped in at some time. Perhaps it fell out of your pocket? I didn't associate this gadget with you as you are...' Cornelius trailed off, politely avoiding reference to Rosie's lack of IT skills.

'Not a whizz with technology.' Rosie finished his sentence for him and continued humbly, 'Don't worry, I know this.' Rosie laughed. 'Ah well, it's good to get it back.' She glanced at the phone with a look of distaste. 'I think,' she added. In truth, she had managed without it. Keen to change the subject from her lack of technological skills, she asked, 'I believe you have Cosmos staying with you for a holiday?'

'Oh yes indeed. He's here with his partner.' As if reading the minds of his companions, he continued. 'There was some talk last year about him being in contact with Fiona, but he hasn't seen her in decades. Indeed, she was just an old flame from the old days in Erin's Glen. I don't know where that rumour came from.' Rosie kept a neutral expression and said nothing. 'But anyway, he's here with Lesley; they've been together for over twenty years, so Fiona was *ancient history,* so to speak...' Cornelius chuckled.

Rosie was about to comment on his little historical joke when the Professor of Celtic History appeared himself. His resemblance to his brother was striking. He spoke with an Anglified accent, 'Oh good day, ladies, such an honour to meet you.' Cosmos gave a little bow of the head. A slightly younger man dressed neatly in jeans and a brightly coloured polo shirt appeared behind Cornelius and Cosmos. They both turned around. Cosmos spoke first, 'Lesley, come and meet Rosie and Mary Jo. They have been instrumental in solving the latest murder in Erin's Glen.'

Just then, a shout went up over the PA system. 'Could the owner of the brown Spaniel dog please come forward now? A *brown spaniel dog*. Thank you.' Rosie glanced down quickly. Ziggy was gone.

Rosie looked across the road and immediately realised what had happened. She was horrified. Ziggy had made a dash for a stall selling cheese, and on the way, he had collided with the May Queen float. In a mad few seconds of mayhem, he had tipped up their floral display, and the May Queen herself was now sprawled on the ground. A local newspaper reporter caught the moment on camera.

Rosie ran to drag him away in disgrace, profusely apologising. She helped the May Queen up off the ground and returned her floral wreath to her. The young woman was shaken but unharmed. Luckily, the rest of the day passed off pleasantly with music and a parade up to the fairy ring. There was a one-minute silence by the oak tree to remember Gerry Macauley, followed by a rendition of his favourite merry tune. Some of the little children began to dance as the fiddles scratched out the happy song. Their innocent exuberance lightened the atmosphere, and all the residents and visitors to Erin's Glen had a day to remember – for all the right reasons.

The next day, *The Erin's Glen Herald* had record sales. A small paragraph on the middle page of the paper confirmed that the Tourist Interpretation Centre would not be built.

However, the *real* reason for the boost in purchases of the newspaper that day was due to its front page photograph and the headline:

Blooming Surprise. May Queen Sensation at Erin's Glen Parade.

Underneath the headline was a picture of Ziggy wearing a lop-sided crown of flowers.

Everyone in the town agreed it was the best front-page news in a long time.

***

You can find more books in the Erin's Glen series at https://www.amazon.com/dp/B0CW18SBXS

If you enjoyed Murder in the Fairy Ring, you will love book three in the series – Murder on Mount Cairn.

Ireland, summer 1991, is the setting for an intriguing tale set in the rural town of Erin's Glen. As the town prepares for its annual Lammas Fair during a rare heatwave, a hiker's perplexing discovery on nearby Mount Cairn casts a cool shadow over the festivities. Tensions rise, and rumours swirl as a group of visiting German students are drawn into the deepening mystery after stumbling upon a second body.

Rosie O'Reilly, the modest parish secretary, takes it upon herself to unravel the truth. With her remarkable photographic memory, Rosie becomes the leading force in untangling a complex web of dark secrets, academic ambitions, greed, and hidden connections, alongside her loyal canine companion, Ziggy, and the energetic nun, Sister Mary Jo, Rosie races against time to uncover the truth before there are more victims. Mrs Blaney, the ever-curious B&B owner, can't resist poking her nose into the latest gossip, adding to the intrigue.

As new characters stir the pot at the Lammas Fair, readers will be taken on a journey brimming with unexpected revelations, set against the timeless charm of Ireland's enchanting countryside. Prepare to be swept away by a story filled with twists and turns that will keep you guessing until the very end.

Murder on Mount Cairn
Chapter One – An Unexpected Discovery

August 1991

Cornelius Quinn strode along purposefully. The morning was calm and still, and the air hung warm and full of expectation. He paused at the foot of Slievecairn, the mountain that dominated the town of Erin's Glen and took in the unusual sight of a perfectly clear blue sky.

As he ascended the side of the mountain with his metal detector in hand, he felt the gentle brush of a light, warm breeze against his bare arms. He took the ascent slowly. Beads of sweat stood out on his forehead. Heat waves were uncommon in Erin's Glen, and he was unaccustomed to the blazing sun. The intense warmth from the previous few days seemed to have been stored in the rocks and boulders, and he sensed their reflected heat against his skin. He leaned against a sheer boulder as he steadied his breathing and wiped his forehead with a handkerchief.

He was keen to get to the top and discover more interesting artefacts. He had found a few old coins, broken jewellery pieces, and a brooch clasp. He thought there might be graves on the mountain and was keen to find out if he was correct. As an antique shop owner and academic, a significant find would bring him accolades and an uptake in business.

The air cooled perceptively as he reached his destination, a flat plateau that was about halfway up the side of the mountain. Cornelius had grown up in Erin's Glen, and he thought back to the days of his youth when he sprinted up Slievecairn. Even then, the mountain had played tricks on his perception of height and distance. He would expect to be close to the top, only to realise he was only a fraction of the way up. 'A bit like life,' he chuckled to himself.

Cornelius felt his heart quicken, stimulated by his exertion and the anticipation of finding something valuable with his metal detector. He would set the machine up when he got to the flat area. He held it inert for now, his other hand gripping a walking stick for support. The mountain was covered with loose rocks and rubble, making the climb a physical challenge.

A few clouds scudded across the sky, and Cornelius smiled to himself again. 'Blue skies don't last long over Erin's Glen,' he thought ruefully. The soft breeze was starting to whip around with more force, and the dapper gentleman quickened his pace, finding renewed energy in the cool wind and motivated by his wish to avoid a drenching. He could detect the salty smell of rain in the air, a scent that always brought back memories of his childhood.

A few loose stones shifted like ball bearings below his feet, and he lost his balance momentarily. It suddenly struck him how isolated he was up here. No one knew he was coming up here, and if he fell and hurt himself, he could lie alone out here for hours -- days maybe. With a sudden sense of concern for his safety, he berated himself for his lack of forethought – he really should have gotten a mobile phone. He paused, regained his balance and took careful, delicate steps upwards.

The plateau was now clearly in sight, and he took a deep breath of gratitude to be up here safely. After setting up his metal detector, he began to walk slowly across the expanse of grass and rocks. Although flatter than the ascent, the ground here continued gradually up the mountain in a slow but vast incline. Rough stones and knobbly rocks littered the ground. There were the remains of an old stone wall and the foundations of a tiny structure, possibly a rough cottage from the distant past or a shelter for a goat or sheep herd from long ago. The wind whipped around Cornelius' legs now. The air was chillier up here. The weather was changing rapidly. From his high vantage point, he could see the next town, Rocksheelan, a few miles away. Behind him, the town of Erin's Glen was waking up. Many had slept poorly due to the unaccustomed heat and would be relieved to open windows and doors to a cooler morning. Cornelius felt detached from the mundane concerns of the town's inhabitants and was content to scan the ground below him. The metal detector in his hand now made a whirring noise and the occasional beep. He moved it across the earth patiently. He couldn't hurry this. He might miss something. In truth, Cornelius enjoyed this quiet, concentrated activity for its own sake. He believed youngsters called it 'being in the zone.' Indeed, he felt like he was gently transported into a more meditative state by his hobby, and he looked forward to this quiet, solitary pastime. The promise of academic accolades appealed to his ego. His mind drifted off to the papers or books he could write about his finds up here. Perhaps an honorary professorship at Trinity, Queen's or maybe at the newer University of Ulster?

Whirr, whirr. Beep, beep.

The machine pushed out its predictable noise. Cornelius moved across the mossy grass, punctuated by rough patches of stone and rock, with calm attention. Out of the corner of his eye, he detected something that shouldn't be there. His heart rate quickened again, and he felt panic creep up his body like a fever. His hands began to shake, and his throat constricted. He did not want to take a second look to confirm what he thought he saw. Like a child, he shut his eyes tight, and although not religious, he said a prayer that he had been mistaken in what he thought he saw. With a deep breath and a dizzying sense of alarm, he forced himself to look again.

Yes, he was now sure of what he saw.

He quickly glanced around. Save for a few seagulls hovering on the updraught at the side of the mountain and the distant bleating of sheep along the hillsides. All was quiet. The sky was now a dull metal grey. Goosebumps came up on his bare arms and legs. Cornelius shivered and walked results towards a tall boulder. He zeroed in on the grim sight – a hand protruding from the earth.

http://books2read.com/erinsglen3

About the author

A.P Ryan grew up in Ireland and attended Queen's University Belfast, where she studied Law, English Literature and Irish History. Her varied career in teaching, waitressing, social work and dog walking has given her ample material for writing. She has been happily married to the man of her dreams for over twenty years and is a proud mum to their grown-up kids. A.P Ryan now lives in a small town in deepest, darkest Devon, but she regularly commutes to Erin's Glen, where she spends many happy hours helping her sleuth unravel mysteries.

You can follow A.P Ryan at http://facebook.com/GlensideBooks

Printed in Dunstable, United Kingdom